David Humphreys

An Essay on the Life of the Honorable Major-General Israel Putnam

Addressed to the state society of the Cincinnati in Connecticut

David Humphreys

An Essay on the Life of the Honorable Major-General Israel Putnam
Addressed to the state society of the Cincinnati in Connecticut

ISBN/EAN: 9783337087432

Printed in Europe, USA, Canada, Australia, Japan

AN ESSAY ON THE LIFE OF THE HONORABLE MAJOR-GENERAL ISRAEL PUTNAM:

Addressed to the State Society of the Cincinnati in Connecticut.

By Col. DAVID HUMPHREYS.

HARTFORD:
PRINTED BY HUDSON AND GOODWIN,
M.DCC.LXXXVIII.

To the Honorable

Col. JEREMIAH WADSWORTH,

PRESIDENT of the STATE SOCIETY of the CINCINNATI in CONNECTICUT, &c. &c.

MY DEAR SIR,

UNAVOIDABLE abſence will prevent me from performing the grateful taſk, aſſigned me by the State Society of the Cincinnati, on the fourth day of July next. Though I cannot perſonally addreſs them, I wiſh to demonſtate by ſome token of affectionate remembrance, the ſenſe I entertain of the honor they have more than once conferred upon me by their ſuffrages.

MEDITATING in what manner to accompliſh this object, it occurred to me, that an attempt to preſerve the actions of General Putnam, in the archives of our State Society, would be acceptable to its members; as they had all ſerved with great ſatisfaction under his immediate orders. An eſſay on the life of a perſon ſo elevated in military rank, and ſo converſant in extraordinary ſcenes, could not be deſtitute of amuſement and inſtruction, and would poſſeſs the advantage of preſenting for imitation a reſpectable model of public and private virtues.

GENERAL Putnam is univerſally acknowledged to have been as brave and as honeſt a man as ever America produced; but the diſtinguiſhing features of his character, and the particular tranſactions of his life are but imperfectly known. He ſeems to have been formed on purpoſe for the age in which he lived. His native courage, unſhaken integrity, and eſtabliſhed reputation as a ſoldier, were neceſſary in the early ſtages of our oppoſition to the deſigns of Great Britain, and gave unbounded confidence to our troops in their firſt conflicts in the field of battle.

THE incloſed manuſcript juſtly claims indulgence for its venial errors, as it is the firſt effort in biography, that has been made on this continent. The attempt, I am conſcious is laudable, whatever may be the failure in point of execution.

I AM happy to find that the Society of the Cincinnati is now generally regarded in a favorable manner. Mankind, with few exceptions, are diſpoſed to do juſtice to the motives on which it was founded. For ourſelves, we can never recall to mind the occaſion, without feeling the moſt tender emotions of friendſhip and ſenſibility. At the diſſolution of the army, when we retired to ſeparate walks of life, from the toils of a ſucceſsful war, in which we had been aſſociated during a very important part of our lives; the pleaſing idea, and the fond hope of meeting once a year, *which gave birth to our fraternal inſtitution*, were neceſſary conſolations to ſooth the pangs, that tore our boſoms at the melancholy hour of parting. When our hands touched, perhaps, for the laſt time and our tongues refuſed to perform their office in bidding farewell, Heaven witneſſed and approved the purity of our intentions in the ardor of our affections. May we perſevere in the union of our friendſhip, and the exertion of our benevolence; regardleſs of the cenſures of jealous ſuſpicion, which charges our deſigns with ſelfiſhneſs, and aſcribes our actions to improper motives; while we realize ſentiments of a nobler nature in our anniverſary feſtivities, and our hearts dilate with an honeſt joy, in opening the hand of beneficence to the indigent widow and unprotected orphan of our departed friends.

I PRAY you, my dear Sir, to preſent my

moſt reſpectful compliments to the members of the Society, and to aſſure them on my part, that whenſoever it ſhall be in my power, I ſhall eſteem it the felicity of my life to attend their anniverſaries.

I HAVE the honor to be, with ſentiments of the higheſt conſideration and eſteem, your moſt obedient and moſt humble ſervant,

D. HUMPHREYS.

Mount Vernon, in Virginia,
June 4th, 1788.

AN

ESSAY

ON THE LIFE OF

GENERAL PUTNAM.

TO treat of recent tranſactions and perſons ſtill living, is always a delicate and frequently a thankleſs office. Yet, while the partiality of friends or the malignity of enemies decides with raſhneſs on every delineation of character, or recital of circumſtances; a conſolation remains that diſtant nations and remoter ages, free from the influence of prejudice or paſſion, will judge with impartiality and appreciate with juſtice. We have fallen upon an æra ſingularly prolific in extraordinary perſonages, and dignified by ſplendid events. Much is expected from the ſelections of the judicious biographer, as well as from the labors of the faithful hiſtorian. Whatever prudential reaſons may now occur to poſtpone the portrait of our own times; the difficulties which oppoſe themſelves to the execution, inſtead of being diminiſhed, will encreaſe with the lapſe of years. Every day will extinguiſh ſome life that was dear to fame, and obliterate the memorial of ſome deed which would have conſtituted the delight and admiration of the world.

So tranſient and indiſtinguiſhable are the traits of character, ſo various and inexplicable the ſprings of action, ſo obſcure and periſhable the remembrance of human affairs, that, unleſs attempts are made to ſketch the picture, while the preſent generation is living, the likeneſs will be forever loſt, or only preſerved by a vague recollection; diſguiſed, perhaps, by the whimſical colorings of a creative imagination.

It will doubtleſs hereafter be an object of regret that thoſe, who, having themſelves been conſpicuous actors on the theatre of public life, and, who in conjunction with a knowlege of facts, poſſeſs abilities to paint thoſe characters and deſcribe thoſe events, which (during the progreſs of the American Revolution) intereſted and aſtoniſhed mankind, ſhould feel an inſuperable reluctance to aſſume the taſk—a taſk, which (if executed with fidelity) muſt, from the dignity of its ſubject, become grateful to the patriots of all nations, and profitable in example to the remoteſt poſterity. Equally ſevere will be the mortification of contemplating the reveries and fictions, which have been ſubſtituted by hacknied writers in the place of hiſtorical facts. Nor ſhould we ſuppreſs our indignation againſt that claſs of profeſſional authors, who, placed in the vale of penury and obſcurity, at an immenſe diſtance from the ſcenes of action and all opportunities of acquiring the neceſſary documents, with inſufferable effrontery, obtrude their fallacious and crude performances on a credulous public. Did the reſult of their lucubrations terminate only in relieving their own diſtreſſes or gratifying their individual vanity, it might be paſſed in ſilent contempt. But the effect is extenſive, permanent and pernicious. The lye,* however improbable or monſtrous, which has once aſſumed the ſemblance of truth, by being often repeated with minute and plauſible particulars, is at length ſo tho-

* The writer had here particularly in his eye, the Rhapſody, palmed upon the public, under the name of a Hiſtory, by a certain Frenchman called D'Auberteiul: Perhaps ſo much falſhood, folly and calumny was never before accumulated in a ſingle performance.

roughly eſtabliſhed, as to obtain univerſal credit, defy contradiction and fruſtrate every effort of refutation. Such is the miſchief, ſuch are the unhappy conſequences on the bewildered mind, that the reader has no alternative, but to become the dupe of his credulity, or diſtruſt the veracity of almoſt all human teſtimony. After having long been the ſport of fiction, he will perhaps probably run into the oppoſite extreme, and give up all confidence in the annals of ancient as well as modern times: and thus the eaſy-believer of fine fables and marvellous ſtories will find, at laſt, his hiſtorical faith change to ſcepticiſm and end in infidelity.

The numerous errors and falſehoods relative to the birth and atchievements of Major General Putnam, which have (at a former period) been circulated with aſſiduity on both ſides of the Atlantic, and the uncertainty which appeared to prevail with reſpect to his real ‡ character, firſt produced the reſo-

‡ The following lines are extracted from a poem, entitled "The Proſpect of America:" written by the late ingenious Dr. Ladd.

"Hail! Putnam! hail, thou venerable name!
"Tho' dark oblivion threats thy mighty fame,
"It threats in vain—for long ſhalt thou be known,
"Who firſt in virtue and in battle ſhone,

lution of writing this essay on his life and induced the editor to obtain * materials from that hero himself. If communications of such authenticity, if personal intimacy as an aid-de-camp to that General, or if subsequent military employments, which afforded access to sources † of intelligence not open to

" When fourscore years had blanch'd thy laurell'd head,
" Strong in thine age, the flame of war was spread."

On which Dr. Ladd made this note :

" The brave Putnam seems to have been almost obscured amidst the glare of succeeding worthies ; but his early and gallant services entitle him to an everlasting remembrance."

Other bards have also asserted the glory of this venerable veteran. In the first concise review of the principal American heroes who signalized themselves in the last war, the same character is thus represented :

" There stood stern Putnam, seam'd with many a scar,
" The veteran honors of an earlier war."

The Vision of Columbus, Book V.

* The editor seizes with eagerness an opportunity of acknowledging his obligations to Dr. Albigence Waldo, who was so obliging as to commit to writing many anecdotes, communicated to him by General Putnam in the course of the present year.

† A multitude of proofs might be produced to demonstrate that military facts cannot always be accurately known but by the commander in chief and his confidential officers. The marquis de Chastelleux (whose opportunity to acquire genuine information, respecting those parts of the American war which he hath casually mentioned, was better than that of any other writer) gives an account of a *grand Forage* which general Heath ordered to be made towards Kingsbridge in the autumn

others, give the writer any advantages; the unbiassed mind will decide how far they exculpate him from the imputations of that officiousness, ignorance and presumption, which

of 1780. The Marquis, who was present when the detachment marched, and to whom General Heath shewed the orders that were given to General Stark, the commanding officer of the expedition, observes that he had never seen, in manuscript or print, more pertinent instructions. Now the fact is, that this detachment, under the pretext of a forage, was intended by the Commander in chief to co-operate with the main army in an attempt against the enemy's posts on York-Island; and that General Heath himself was then ignorant of the real design. The Commander in Chief spent a whole campaign in ripening this project. Boats, mounted on traveling carriages, were kept constantly with the army. The marquis de la Fayette, at the head of the Light Infantry, was to have made the attack in the night on fort Washington. The period chosen for this enterprise was the very time, when the army were to break up their camp and march into winter-quarters: so that the Commander in Chief, moving in the dusk of the evening, would have been on the banks of the Hudson, with his whole force, to have supported the attack. The cautious manner in which the co-operation on the part of the troops sent by General Heath, on the pretended forage, was to have been conducted, will be understood from the following secret instructions.

" To Brigadier General STARK.

Head Quarters Passaic Falls Nov. 21, 1780.

" SIR,

" Colonel Humphreys, one of my aides de camp, is " charged by me with orders of a private and particu-" lar nature, which he is to deliver to you, and which in others have been reprehended with ſeverity. He only wiſhes that a premature and unfavorable conſtruction may not be formed of his motive or object. Should this eſſay

" you are to obey. He will inform you of the neceſſity " of this mode of communication.

" I am, Sir, &c.

" Geo. Waſhington."

" *To Lieut. Col. David Humphreys, A. D. Camp.*

" SIR,

" You are immediately to proceed to Weſt-Point and " communicate the buſineſs committed to you, *in confi-* " *dence*, to Major General Heath, and to no other per- " ſon whatſoever; from thence you will repair to the " detachment at the White Plains, on Friday next, ta- " king meaſures to prevent their leaving that place, be- " fore you get to them. And in the courſe of the ſuc- " ceeding night you may inform the commanding offi- " cer of the enterprize in contemplation againſt the en- " emy's poſts on York Iſland.

" As the troops are conſtantly to lie on their arms, no " previous notice ſhould be given; but they may be " put in motion preciſely at 4 o'clock, and commence " a ſlow and regular march to King's Bridge, until they " ſhall diſcover or be informed of the concerted ſignals " being made—when the march muſt be preſſed with " the greateſt rapidity. Parties of horſe ſhould be ſent " forward to keep a look out for the ſignals.

" Although the main body ought to be kept com- " pact, patroles of horſe and light parties might be ſent " towards Eaſt and Weſt Cheſter: and upon the ſignals " being diſcovered, Sheldon's regiment and the Con- " necticut State troops (which may alſo be put in mo- " tion as ſoon as the orders can be communicated after " 4 o'clock) ſhould be puſhed forward to intercept any have any influence in correcting miſtakes, or reſcuing from oblivion the actions of that diſtinguiſhed Veteran; ſhould it create an emulation to copy his domeſtic, manly and

" of the enemy, who may attempt to gain Frog's Neck, " and to cut off the Refugee-corps at Morriſſania. A " few men, with ſome addreſs, may ſpread ſuch an a- " larm as to prevent an attempt of the enemy to re- " treat to Frog's Neck, from an apprehenſion of ſur- " rounding parties.

" You will communicate theſe inſtructions to the com- " manding officer of the detachment, who, upon his " approach to King's Bridge, will receive orders from me " as early as poſſible.

" Should the ſignals not be diſcovered, the troops " will halt at leaſt ſix miles from the bridge, until fur- " ther intelligence can be obtained.

" The abſolute neceſſity of the moſt perfect ſecrecy is " the occaſion of communicating my orders through " this channel."

Given at Head-Quarters, Paſſaic Falls,
this 22d day of Nov. 1780,
Geo. Waſhington.

Never was a plan better arranged: and never did circumſtances promiſe more ſure or complete ſucceſs. The Britiſh were not only unalarmed, but our own troops were likewiſe entirely miſguided in their expectations. The accidental intervention of ſome veſſels prevented at this time the attempt: which was more than once reſumed afterwards. Notwithſtanding this favorite project was not ultimately effected, it was evidently not leſs bold in conception or feaſible in accompliſhment, than that attempted ſo ſucceſsfully at Trenton; or than that, which was brought to ſo glorious an iſſue in the ſucceſsful ſiege of York-Town.

heroic virtues; or ſhould it prompt ſome more ſkilful hand to pourtray the illuſtrious groupe of Patriots, Sages and Heroes, who have guided our counſels, fought our battles and adorned the memorable Epocha of Independence, it will be an ample compenſation for the trouble and excite a conſolatory reflection through every viciſſitude of life.

ISRAEL PUTNAM, who through a regular gradation of promotion became the ſenior Major General in the army of the United States, and next in rank to General Waſhington, was born at Salem in the Province, now State, of Maſſachuſetts, on the 7th day of January 1718. His father, Capt. Joſeph Putnam was the ſon of Mr. John Putnam, who with two brothers came from the ſouth

It is true the Marquis de Chaſtellux, whoſe profeſſional knowledge and fountain-head intelligence have enabled him to deſcribe ſeveral actions better than they are elſewhere deſcribed, ſpeaks in this inſtance of an ulterior object: and ſays that ſecrets were preſerved more inviolably in the American than in the French army. His words are:

"C'eſt que le ſecret eſt garde tres exactement a "l'armee Americaine; peu de perſonnes ont "part a la confiance du Chef, et en general on y "parle moins que dans les armees Francoiſes des op- "erations de la guerre, et de ce que l'on appelle "chez nous *les Nouvelles*."

of England and were among the firſt ſettlers of Salem.

WHEN we thus behold a perſon, from the humble walks of life, ſtarting unnoticed in the career of fame, and, by an undeviating progreſs through a life of honor, arriving at the higheſt dignity in the ſtate; curioſity is ſtrongly excited, and philoſophy loves to trace the path of glory from the cradle of obſcurity to the ſummit of elevation.

ALTHOUGH our anceſtors, the firſt ſettlers of this land, amidſt the extreme preſſure of poverty and danger, early inſtituted ſchools for the education of youths, deſigned for the learned profeſſions; yet it was thought ſufficient to inſtruct thoſe deſtined to labor on the earth, in reading, writing and ſuch rudiments of arithmetic, as might be requiſite for keeping the accounts of their little tranſactions with each other. Few farmer's ſons had more advantages, none leſs. In this ſtate of mediocrity it was the lot of young Putnam to be placed. His early inſtruction was not conſiderable, and the active ſcenes of life, in which he was afterwards engaged, prevented the opportunity of great literary improvement. His numerous original letters, though deficient in ſcholaſtic accuracy, always diſplay the goodneſs of his heart, and frequently the ſtrength of his native genius. He had a certain laconic mode of expreſſion, and an unaffected epigrammatic turn, which characteriſed moſt of his writings.

To compenſate partially for the deficiency of education (though nothing can remove or counterbalance the inconveniences experienced from it in public life) he derived from his parents the ſource of innumerable advantages in the ſtamina of a vigorous conſtitution. Nature, liberal in beſtowing on him bodily ſtrength, hardineſs and activity, was, by no means, parſimonious in mental endowments. While we leave the qualities of the underſtanding to be developed in the proceſs of life, it may not be improper, in this place, to deſignate ſome of the circumſtances, which were calculated to diſtinguiſh him afterwards as a partizan officer.

Courage, enterprize, activity and perſeverance were the firſt characteriſtics of his mind. There is a kind of mechanical courage, the offspring of pride, habit or diſcipline, that may puſh a coward not only to perform his duty, but even to venture on acts of heroiſm. Putnam's courage was of a different ſpecies. His undaunted feelings depended, leſs than the feelings of moſt others, on external objects, adventitious aids, or the influence of example. He ſtood alone, and collected within himſelf, always poſſeſſed intrepidity equal to the occaſion. His bravery, that appears to have been conſtitutional, never for a moment deſerted him in the trying ſituations, to which his life was often expoſed. It was a ſpecies of cool, deliberate fortitude, not affected by the paroxiſm of enthuſiaſm, or the phrenzy of deſperation. It was ever attended with a ſerenity of ſoul, a clearneſs of conception, a degree of ſelf-poſſeſſion and a ſuperiority to all the viciſſitudes of fortune, entirely diſtinct from any thing that can be produced by the ferment of blood, and flutter of ſpirits, which, not unfrequently, precipitate men to action, when ſtimulated by intoxication or ſome other tranſient exhilaration. The heroic character, thus founded on conſtitution and animal ſpirits, cheriſhed by education and ideas of perſonal freedom, confirmed by temperance and habits of exerciſe, was completed by the dictate of reaſon, the love of his country and an invincible ſenſe of duty. Such were the qualities and principles, that enabled him to meet unappalled the blaſts of adverſity, and to paſs in triumph through the furnace of affliction.

His disposition was as frank and generous, as his mind was fearless and independent. He disguised nothing; indeed he seemed incapable of disguise. Perhaps, in the intercourse he was ultimately obliged to have with an artful world, his sincerity, on some occasions, outwent his discretion. Although he had too much suavity in his nature to commence a quarrel, he had too much sensibility not to feel, and too much honor not to resent an intended insult. The first time he went to Boston, he was insulted for his rusticity by a boy of twice his size and age; after bearing the sarcasms until his patience was worn out, he challenged, engaged and vanquished his unmannerly antagonist, to the great diversion of a crowd of spectators. While a stripling his ambition was to perform the labor of a man, and to excel in athletic diversions. In that rude, but masculine age, whenever the village-youth assembled on their usual occasions of festivity; pitching the bar, running, leaping and wrestling were favorite amusements. At such gymnastic exercises (in which during the heroic times of ancient Greece and Rome, conquest was considered as the promise of future military fame) he bore the palm from almost every ring.

Before the refinements of luxury and the consequent increase of expences had rendered the maintenance of a family inconvenient or burdensome in America, the sexes entered into matrimony at an early age. Competence, attainable by all, was the limit of pursuit. After the hardships of making a new settlement were overcome and the evils of penury removed, the inhabitants enjoyed, in the lot of equality, innocence and security, scenes equally delightful with those, pictured by the glowing imagination of the poets, in their favorite pastoral life or fabulous golden age. Indeed the condition of mankind was never more enviable. Neither disparity of age and fortune, nor schemes of ambition and grandeur, nor the pride and avarice of high-minded and mercenary parents, interposed those obstacles to the union of congenial souls, which frequently in more polished society prevent, imbitter or destroy all the felicity of the connubial state. Mr. Putnam before he attained the twenty-first year of his age, married Miss Pope, daughter of Mr. John Pope of Salem, by whom he had ten children, seven of whom are still living. He lost the wife of his youth in 1764. Some time after he married Mrs. Gardiner, widow of the late Mr. Gardiner of Gardiker's Iſland, by whom he had no iſſue. She died in 1777.

In the year 1739 he removed from Salem to Pomfret, an inland fertile town in Connecticut, forty miles eaſt of Hartford: having here purchaſed a conſiderable tract of land, he applied himſelf ſucceſsfully to agriculture.

The firſt years, on a new farm, are not, however, exempt from diſaſters and diſappointments, which can only be remedied by ſtubborn and patient induſtry. Our farmer, ſufficiently occupied in building an houſe and barn, felling woods, making fences, ſowing grain, planting orchards and taking care of his ſtock, had to encounter, in turn, the calamities occaſioned by drought in ſummer, blaſt in harveſt, loſs of cattle in winter, and the deſolation of his ſheep-fold by wolves. In one night he had ſeventy fine ſheep and goats killed, beſides many lambs and kids wounded. This havoc was committed by a ſhe-wolf, which, with her annual whelps, had for ſeveral years infeſted the vicinity. The young were commonly deſtroyed by the vigilance of the hunters, but the old one was too ſagacious to come within reach of gunſhot: upon being cloſely purſued ſhe would generally fly to the weſtern woods, and return the next winter with another litter of whelps.

This Wolf, at length, became ſuch an intolerable nuiſance, that Mr. Putnam entered into a combination with five of his neighbors to hunt alternately until they could deſtroy her. Two, by rotation, were to be conſtantly in purſuit. It was known, that, having loſt the toes from one foot, by a ſteel-trap, ſhe made one track ſhorter than the other. By this veſtige, the purſuers recognized, in a light ſnow, the route of this pernicious animal. Having followed her to Connecticut river and found ſhe had turned back in a direct courſe towards Pomfret, they immediately returned, and by ten o'clock the next morning the blood-hounds had driven her into a den, about three miles diſtant from the houſe of Mr. Putnam: The people ſoon collected with dogs, guns, ſtraw, fire and ſulphur to attack the common enemy. With this apparatus ſeveral unſucceſsful efforts were made to force her from the den. The hounds came back badly wounded and refuſed to return. The ſmoke of blazing ſtraw had no effect. Nor did the fumes of burnt brimſtone, with which the cavern was filled, compel her to quit the retirement. Wearied with ſuch fruitleſs attempts (which had brought the time to ten o'clock at night) Mr. Putnam tried once more to make his dog enter, but in vain; he propofed to his negro man to go down into the cavern and fhoot the Wolf: the negro declined the hazardous fervice. Then it was that their mafter, angry at the difappointment, and declaring that he was afhamed to have a coward in his family, refolved himfelf to deftroy the ferocious beaft, left fhe fhould efcape through fome unknown fiffure of the rock. His neighbors ftrongly remonftrated againft the perilous enterprize: but he, knowing that wild animals were intimidated by fire, and having provided feveral ftrips of birch-bark, the only combuftible material which he could obtain, that would afford light in this deep and darkfome cave, prepared for his defcent. Having, accordingly, divefted himfelf of his coat and waiftcoat, and having a long rope faftened round his legs, by which he might be pulled back, at a concerted fignal, he entered head foremoft, with the blazing torch in his hand.

The aperture of the den, on the eaft fide of a very high ledge of rocks, is about two feet fquare; from thence it defcends obliquely fifteen feet, then running horizontally about ten more, it afcends gradually fixteen feet towards its termination. The fides of this ſubterraneous cavity are compoſed of ſmooth and ſolid rocks, which ſeem to have been divided from each other by ſome former earthquake. The top and bottom are alſo of ſtone, and the entrance, in winter, being covered with ice, is exceedingly ſlippery. It is in no place high enough for a man to raiſe himſelf upright: nor in any part more than three feet in width.

HAVING groped his paſſage to the horizontal part of the den, the moſt terrifying darkneſs appeared in front of the dim circle of light afforded by his torch. It was ſilent as the houſe of death. None but monſters of the deſert had ever before explored this ſolitary manſion of horror. He, cautiouſly proceeding onward, came to the aſcent; which he ſlowly mounted on his hands and knees until he diſcovered the glaring eye-balls of the wolf, who was ſitting at the extremity of the cavern. Started at the ſight of fire, ſhe gnaſhed her teeth and gave a ſullen growl. As ſoon as he had made the neceſſary diſcovery, he kicked the rope as a ſignal for pulling him out. The people, at the mouth of the den, who had liſtened with painful anxiety, hearing the growling of the wolf and ſuppoſing their friend to be in the moſt imminent danger, drew him forth with ſuch celerity that his ſhirt was ſtripped over his head and his ſkin ſeverely lacerated. After he had adjuſted his cloaths and loaded his gun with nine buck-ſhot, holding a torch in one hand and the muſquet in the other, he deſcended a ſecond time. When he drew nearer than before, the Wolf, aſſuming a ſtill more fierce and terrible appearance, howling, rolling her eyes, ſnapping her teeth, and dropping her head between her legs, was evidently in the attitude and on the point of ſpringing at him. At the critical inſtant he levelled and fired at her head. Stunned with the ſhock and ſuffocated with the ſmoke, he immediately found himſelf drawn out of the cave. But having refreſhed himſelf and permitted the ſmoke to diſſipate, he went down the third time. Once more he came within ſight of the Wolf, who appearing very paſſive, he applied the torch to her noſe; and perceiving her dead, he took hold of her ears, and then kicking the rope (ſtill tied round his legs) the people above, with no ſmall exultation, dragged them both out together.

I HAVE offered theſe facts in greater detail, becauſe they contain a diſplay of character; and becauſe they have been erroneouſly related in ſeveral European publications, and very much mutilated in the hiſtory of Connecticut, a work as replete with falſehood as deſtitute of genius, lately printed in London.

Prosperity, at length, began to attend the agricultural affairs of Mr. Putnam. He was acknowledged to be a ſkilful and indefatigable manager. His fields were moſtly encloſed with ſtone walls. His crops commonly ſucceeded, becauſe the land was well tilled and manured. His paſtures and meadows became luxuriant. His cattle were of the beſt breed and in good order. His garden and fruit-trees prolific. With the avails of the ſurpluſage of his produce foreign articles were purchaſed. Within doors he found the compenſation of his labors in the plenty of excellent proviſions, as well as in the happineſs of domeſtic ſociety.

A more particular deſcription of his tranſition from narrow to eaſy circumſtances might be given; but the mind, that ſhall have acquired an idea of the habits of labor and ſimplicity, to which the induſtrious coloniſts were accuſtomed, will readily ſupply the omiſſion. The effect of this gradual acquiſition of property, generally favorable to individual virtue and public felicity, ſhould not however be paſſed over in ſilence. If there is ſomething faſcinating in the charms of a country life, from the contemplation of beautiful landſcapes; there is likewiſe ſomething elevating to the ſoul, in the conſciouſneſs of being lord of the ſoil and having the power of creating them. The man can ſcarcely be guilty of a ſordid action, or even deſcend to an ungenerous thought, who, removed from the apprehenſion of want, ſees his farm daily meliorating and aſſuming whatever appearance he pleaſes to preſcribe. This ſituation converts the farmer into a ſpecies of rural philoſopher, by inſpiring an honeſt pride in his rank as a freeman, flattering the natural propenſity for perſonal independence, and nouriſhing an unlimited hoſpitality and philanthropy in his ſocial character.

But the time had now arrived, which was to turn the inſtruments of huſbandry into weapons of hoſtility, and to exchange the hunting of wolves, who had ravaged the ſheep-folds, for the purſuit after Savages who had deſolated the frontiers. Mr. Putnam was about 37 years old, when the war between England and France, which preceded the laſt, broke out in America. His reputation muſt have been favorably known to the government, ſince among the firſt troops that were levied by Connecticut, in 1755, he was appointed to the command of a company in Lyman's regiment of Provincials. I have mentioned his age at this period expreſsly to obviate a prevalent opinion, that he was far advanced in life when he commenced his military ſervice.

As he was extremely popular, he found no difficulty in enliſting his complement of recruits from the moſt hardy, enterprizing and reſpectable young men of his neighborhood. The regiment joined the army, at the opening of the campaign, not far diſtant from Crown-Point. Soon after his arrival in camp, he became intimately connected with the famous partizan Captain, afterwards, Major Rogers; with whom he was frequently aſſociated in traverſing the wilderneſs, reconnoitring the enemy's lines, gaining intelligence, and taking ſtraggling priſoners; as well as in beating up the quarters and ſurpriſing the advanced pickets of their army. For theſe operations a corps of rangers, was formed from the irregulars. The firſt time Rogers and Putnam were detached with a party of theſe light troops it was the fortune of the latter to preſerve, with his own hand, the life of the former, and to cement their friendſhip with the blood of one of their enemies. The object of this expedition was to obtain an accurate knowledge of the poſition and ſtate of the works at Crown Point. It was impracticable to approach with their party near enough for this purpoſe, without being diſcovered. Alone, the undertaking was ſufficiently hazardous, on account of the ſwarms of hoſtile Indians who infeſted the woods. Our two partizans, however, left all their men at a convenient diſtance, with ſtrict orders to continue concealed until their return. Having thus cautiouſly taken their arrangements, they advanced with the profoundeſt ſilence, in the evening; and lay, during the night, contiguous to the fortreſs. Early in the morning, they approached ſo cloſe as to be able to give ſatisfactory information, to the general who had ſent them, on the ſeveral points to which their attention had been directed: but Captain Rogers, being at a little diſtance from Captain Putnam, fortuitouſly met a ſtout Frenchman, who inſtantly ſeized his fuzee with one hand and with the other attempted to ſtab him, while he called to an adjacent guard for aſſiſtance. The guard anſwered. Putnam, perceiving the imminent danger of his friend, and that no time was to be loſt or farther alarm given by firing, ran rapidly to them, while they were yet ſtruggling, and with the butt-end of his piece laid the Frenchman dead at his feet. The partizans, to elude purſuit, precipitated their flight, joined the party and returned without loſs to the encampment. Not many occaſions occurred for partizans to diſplay their talents in the courſe of this ſummer. The war was chequered with various fortune in different quarters—ſuch as the total defeat of General Braddock, and the ſplendid victory of Sir William Johnſon over the French troops commanded by the Baron Dieſkau. The brilliancy of this ſucceſs was neceſſary to conſole the Americans for the diſgrace of that diſaſter. Here I might, indeed, take a pride in contraſting the conduct of the Britiſh Regulars, who had been ambuſcaded on the Monongahela; with that of the Provincials (under Johnſon) who, having been attacked in their lines, gallantly repulſed the enemy and took their General priſoner: did I conſider myſelf at liberty to ſwell this eſſay with reflections on events, in which Putnam not directly concerned. The time for which the colonial troops engaged to ſerve, terminated with the campaign. Putnam was re-appointed and again took the field in 1756.

Few are ſo ignorant of war as not to know,

that military adventures, in the night, are always extremely liable to accidents. Captain Putnam, having been commanded to reconnoitre the enemy's camp at *the Ovens*, near *Ticonderoga*, took the brave Lieutenant Robert Durkee as his companion. In attempting to execute these orders, he narrowly missed being taken himself in the first instance and killing his friend in the second. It was customary for the British and Provincial troops to place their fires round their camp, which frequently exposed them to the enemy's scouts and patroles. A contrary practice, then unknown in the English army, prevailed among the French and Indians. The plan was much more rational; they kept their fires in the centre, lodged their men circularly at a distance and posted their centinels in the surrounding darkness. Our partizans approached the camp—and supposing the centries were within the circle of fires, crept upon their hands and knees with the greatest possible caution, until, to their utter astonishment, they found themselves in the thickest of the enemy. The centinels, discovering them, fired and slightly wounded Durkee in the thigh. He and Putnam had no alternative. They fled. The latter, being foremost and scacely able to see his hand before him, soon plunged into a clay-pit. Durkee, almoſt at the identical moment, came tumbling after. Putnam, by no means pleaſed at finding a companion and believing him to be one of the enemy, lifted his tomahawk to give the deadly blow—when Durkee, (who had followed ſo cloſely as to know him) enquired whether he had eſcaped unhurt. Captain Putnam, inſtantly recognizing the voice, dropped his weapon: and both, ſpringing from the pit, made good their retreat to the neighboring ledges, amidſt a ſhower of random ſhot. There they betook themſelves to a large log, by the ſide of which they lodged, the remainder of the night. Before they lay down, Captain Putnam ſaid he had a little rum in his canteen, which could never be more acceptable or neceſſary; but on examining the canteen, which hung under his arm, he found the enemy had pierced it with their balls and that there was not a drop of liquor left. The next day he found fourteen bullet holes in his blanket.

In the ſame ſummer a body of the enemy, conſiſting of 600 men, attacked the baggage and proviſion waggons at a place called the half-way brook; it being equidiſtant from Fort Edward, and the ſouth end of lake George. Having killed the oxen and plundered the waggons, they retreated with their booty without having met with ſuch reſiſtance as might have been expected from the ſtrength of the eſcort. General Webb, upon receiving intelligence of this diſaſter, ordered the Captains Putnam and Rogers " to take 100 " volunteers in boats, with two wall-pieces " and two blunderbuſſes, and to proceed " down lake George to a certain point: there " to leave the batteaux under a proper guard, " and thence to croſs by land ſo as to harraſs " and if practicable intercept the retreating " enemy at the narrows." Theſe orders were executed with ſo much punctuality, that the party arrived at the deſtined place half an hour before the hoſtile boats came in view. Here they waited, under cover, until the enemy (ignorant of theſe proceedings) entered the narrows with their batteaux loaded with plunder. Then the volunteers poured upon them volley after volley, killed many of the oarſmen, ſunk a number of the batteaux, and would ſoon have deſtroyed the whole body of the enemy, had not the unuſual precipitancy of their paſſage (favored by the wind) carried them through the narrows into the wide part of South Bay; where they were out of the reach of muſquet ſhot. The ſhattered remnant of the little fleet ſoon arrived at Ticonderoga and gave information that Putnam and Rogers were at the narrows. A fresh party was instantly detached to cut them in pieces, on their return to Fort Edward. Our partizans, sensible of the probability of such an attempt, and being full twenty miles from their boats, strained every nerve to reach them as soon as possible; which they effected the same night. Next day, when they had returned as far as Sabbathday Point, they discovered, on shore, the before mentioned detachment of 300 men, who had passed them in the night, and who now, on perceiving our party, took to their boats with the greatest alacrity, and rowed out to give battle. They advanced in line, maintaining a good mein and felicitating themselves upon the prospect of an easy conquest, from the great superiority of their numbers. Flushed with these expectations, they were permitted to come within pistol-shot before a gun was fired. At once, the wall-pieces and blunderbusses, which had been brought to rake them in the most vulnerable point, were discharged. As no such reception had been foreseen, the assailants were thrown into the utmost disorder. Their terror and confusion were greatly encreased by a well-directed and most destructive fire of the small arms. The larger pieces being reloaded, without annoyance, continued alternately with the musquetry to make dreadful havoc, until the rout was completed and the enemy driven back to Ticònderoga. In this action, one of the bark canoes contained twenty Indians, of whom fifteen were killed. Great numbers, from other boats, both of French and Indians were seen to fall overboard: but the account of their total loss could never be ascertained. Rogers and Putnam had but one man killed and two slightly wounded. They now landed on the point and having refreshed their men at leisure, returned in good order to the British camp.

Soon after these rencounters, a singular kind of race was run by our nimble-footed Provincial and an active young Frenchman. The liberty of each was by turns at stake. General Webb, wanting a prisoner for the sake of intelligence, sent Capt. Putnam with five men to procure one. The Captain concealed himself near the road which leads from Ticonderoga to the Ovens. His men seemed fond of shewing themselves, which unsoldierlike conduct he prohibited with the severest reprehension. This rebuke they imputed to unnecessary fear. The observation is as true as vulgar, that persons, distinguishable for temerity when there is no apparent danger, are generally poltroons whenever danger approaches. They had not lain long, in the high graſs, before a Frenchman and an Indian paſſed—the Indian was conſiderably in advance. As ſoon as the former had gone by, Putnam, relying on the fidelity of his men, ſprang up, ran and ordered them to follow. After runinng about thirty rods, he ſeized the Frenchman by the ſhoulders and forced him to ſurrender : But his priſoner, looking round, perceiving no other enemy and knowing the Indian would be ready in a moment to aſſiſt him, began to make an obſtinate reſiſtance. Putnam, finding himſelf betrayed by his men into a perilous dilemma, let go his hold, ſtepped back and ſnapped his piece, which was levelled at the Frenchman's breaſt. It miſſed fire. Upon this, he thought it moſt prudent to retreat. The Frenchman, in turn, chaſed him back to his men, who, at laſt raiſed themſelves from the graſs ; which his purſuer, eſpying in good time for himſelf, made his eſcape. Putnam, mortified that theſe men had fruſtrated his ſucceſs, diſmiſſed them with diſgrace ; and, not long after accompliſhed his object. Such little feats, as the capture of a ſingle priſoner, may be of infinitely more conſequence than ſome, who are unacquainted with military affairs, would be apt to imagine. In a country covered with woods, like that part of America then the ſeat of war, the difficulty of procuring and the importance of poſſeſſing good intelligence can ſcarcely be conceived even by European commanders. They, however, who know its value, will not appreciate lightly the ſervices of an able partizan.

Nothing, worthy of remark, happened during this campaign except the loſs of Oſwego. That Fort, which had been built by General Shirley to protect the peltry trade, cover the country on the Mohawk River and facilitate an invaſion of Canada by Frontenac and Niagara, fell into the hands of the enemy with a garriſon of ſixteen hundred men and one hundred pieces of cannon.

The active ſervices of Captain Putnam on every occaſion attracted the admiration of the public, and induced the Legiſlature of Connecticut to promote him to a majority in 1757.

Lord Loudon was then Commander in Chief of the Britiſh forces in America. The expedition againſt Crown Point, which from the commencement of hoſtilities had been in contemplation, ſeemed to give place to a more important operation that was meditated againſt Louiſbourg. But the arrival of the Breſt ſquadron at that place prevented the attempt; and the loſs of Fort William-Henry ſerved to clafs this with the two former unfuccefsful campaigns. It was rumoured and partially credited at the time, that General Webb, who commanded in the northern department, had early intimation of the movement of the French army, and might have effectually fuccoured the garrifon. The fubfequent facts will place the affair in its proper light.

A FEW days before the feige, Major Putnam, with two hundred men, efcorted General Webb from Fort Edward to Fort William-Henry. The object was to examine the ftate of this fortification, which ftood at the fouthern extremity of Lake George. Several abortive attempts having been made by Major Rogers and others in the night feafon, Major Putnam propofed to go down the lake in open day-light, land at Northweft-Bay and tarry on fhore, until he could make fatisfactory difcovery of the enemy's actual fituation at Ticonderoga and the adjacent pofts. The plan (which he fuggefted) of landing with only five men and fending back the boats, to prevent detection, was deemed too hazardous by the General. At length, however, he was permitted to proceed with eighteen volunteers in three whale boats: but before he arrived at Northweft-Bay he difcovered a body of men on an Ifland. Immediately upon this, he left two boats to fiſh at a diſtance, that they might not occaſion an alarm, and returned himſelf with the information. The General, ſeeing him rowing back with great velocity, in a ſingle boat, concluded the others were captured and ſent a ſkiff with orders for him alone to come on ſhore. After adviſing the General of the circumſtances, he urged the expediency of returning to make further diſcoveries and bring off the boats. Leave was reluctantly given. He found his people, and, paſſing ſtill onward, diſcovered (by the aid of a good perſpective glaſs) a large army in motion. By this time ſeveral of the advanced canoes had nearly ſurrounded him, but, by the ſwiftneſs of his whale-boats, he eſcaped through the midſt of them. On his return he informed the General minutely of all he had ſeen, and intimated his conviction that the expedition muſt obviouſly be deſtined againſt Fort William-Henry. That Commander, ſtrictly enjoining ſilence on the ſubject, directed him to put his men under an oath of ſecrecy and to prepare, without loſs of time, to return to the Head Quarters of the Army. Major Putnam obſerved "he hoped "his Excellency did not intend to neglect ſo "fair an opportunity of giving battle, ſhould "the enemy preſume to land"—"What do "you think we ſhould do here," replied the

General. Accordingly the next day he returned and the day after Colonel Monro was ordered from Fort Edward, with his regiment, to reinforce the garriſon. That officer took with him all his rich baggage and camp equipage, notwithſtanding Major Putnam's advice to the contrary. The day following his arrival, the enemy landed and beſieged the place.

The Marquis de Montcalm, Commander in Chief for the French in Canada (intending to take advantage of the abſence of a large proportion of the Britiſh force, which he underſtood to be employed under Lord Loudon againſt Louiſbourg) had aſſembled whatever men could be ſpared from Ticonderoga, Crown Point and the other garriſons; with theſe he had combined a conſiderable corps of Canadians and a larger body of Indians than had ever before been collected: making in the whole an army of nearly eight thouſand men. Our garriſon conſiſted of twenty-five hundred and was commanded by Colonel Monro, a very gallant officer; who found the means of ſending expreſs after expreſs to General Webb, with an account of his ſituation and the moſt preſſing ſolicitation for ſuccour. In the mean time, the army at Fort Edward, which originally amounted to about four thousand, had been considerably augmented by Johnson's troops and the militia. On the 8th or 9th day after the landing of the French, General Johnson (in consequence of repeated applications) was suffered to march for the relief of the garrison, with all the Provincials, Militia and Putnam's Rangers: but before they had proceeded three miles, the order was countermanded and they returned. M. de Montcalm informed Major Putnam when a prisoner in Canada, that one of his running Indians saw and reported this movement; and, upon being questioned relatively to the numbers, answered in their figurative style, "*If you can count the leaves on the trees, you can count them.*" In effect, the operations of the siege was suspended and preparations made for re-imbarking, when another of the runners reported that the detachment had gone back. The Marquis de Montcalm, provided with a good train of artillery, meeting with no annoyance from the British army, and but inconsiderable interruption from the garrison, accelerated his approaches so rapidly as to obtain possession of the Fort, in a short time after completing the investiture. An intercepted letter from General Webb, advising the surrender, was sent into the Fort to Colonel Monro by the French General.

The garrison engaged not to serve for eighteen months and were permitted to march out with the honors of war. But the Savages regarded not the capitulation, nor could they be restrained, by the utmost exertion of the Commanding Officer, from committing the most outrageous acts of cruelty. They stripped and plundered all the prisoners, and murdered great numbers in cold blood. Those, who escaped by flight or the protection of the French, arrived in a forlorn condition at Fort Edward: Among these was the Commandant of the Garrison.

The day succeeding this deplorable scene of carnage and barbarity, Major Putnam having been dispatched with his Rangers, to watch the motions of the enemy, came to the shore, when their rear was scarcely beyond the reach of musquet shot. They had carried off all the cannon, stores and water-craft. The Fort was demolished. The barracks, the out-houses and suttlers booths were heaps of ruins. The fires, not yet extinct, and the smoke, offensive from the mucilaginous nature of the fuel, but illy concealed innumerable fragments of human skulls and bones, and, in some instances carcases half-consumed. Dead bodies, weltering in blood, were every where to be seen, violated with all the wanton mutilations of ſavage ingenuity. More than one hundred women, ſome with their brains ſtill oozing from the battered heads, others with their whole hair wrenched collectively with the ſkin from the bloody ſkulls, and many (with their throats cut) moſt inhumanly ſtabbed and butchered; lay ſtripped entirely naked, with their bowels torn out, and afforded a ſpectacle too horrible for deſcription.

Not long after this misfortune, General Lyman ſucceeded to the command of Fort Edward. He reſolved to ſtrengthen it. For this purpoſe one hundred and fifty men were employed in cutting timber. To cover them, Captain Little was poſted (with fifty Britiſh Regulars) at the head of a thick ſwamp about one hundred rods eaſtward of the Fort —to which his communication lay over a tongue of land, formed on the one ſide by the ſwamp and by a creek on the other.

One morning, at day break, a Centinel ſaw indiſtinctly ſeveral birds, as he conceived, come from the ſwamp and fly over him with incredible ſwiftneſs. While he was ruminating on theſe wonderful birds and endeavoring to form ſome idea of their color, ſhape and ſize, an arrow buried itſelf in the limb of a tree juſt above his head. He now diſcov ered the quality, and deſign of theſe winged meſſengers of fate, and gave the alarm. Inſtantly the working party began to retreat along the defile. A large body of Savages, had concealed themſelves in the moraſs before the guard was poſted, were attempting in this way to kill the centinel without noiſe, with deſign to ſurprize the whole party. Finding the alarm given, they ruſhed from the covert, ſhot and tomahawked thoſe who were neareſt at hand, and preſſed hard on the remainder of the unarmed fugitives. Captain Little flew to their relief, and, by pouring on the Indians a well-timed fire, checked the purſuit and enabled ſuch of the fatigue-men as did not fall in the firſt onſet, to retire to the Fort. Thither he ſent for aſſiſtance, his little party being almoſt over-powered by numbers. But the Commandant, imagining that the main body of the enemy were approaching for a general aſſault, called in his out-poſts and ſhut the gates.

Major Putnam lay, with his Rangers, on an Iſland adjacent to the Fort. Having heard the muſquetry and learned that his friend Captain Little was in the utmoſt peril, he plunged into the river at the head of his corps and waded through the water towards the place of engagement. This brought him ſo near to the Fort, that General Lyman, apprized of his deſign and unwilling that the lives of a few more brave men ſhould be expoſed to what he deemed inevitable deſtruction, mounted the parapet and ordered him to proceed no farther. The Major only took time to make the beſt ſhort apology he could and marched on. This is the only inſtance in the whole courſe of his military ſervice, wherein he did not pay the ſtricteſt obedience to orders; and in this inſtance his motive was highly commendable. But when ſuch conduct, even if ſanctified by ſucceſs, is paſſed over with impunity, it demonſtrates that all is not right in the military ſyſtem. In a diſciplined army, ſuch as that of the United States became under General Waſhington, an officer guilty of a ſlighter violation of orders, however elevated in rank or meritorious in ſervice, would have been brought before the bar of a Court Martial. Were it not for the ſeductive tendency of a brave man's example, I might have been ſpared the mortification of making theſe remarks on the conduct of an officer, whoſe diſtinguiſhing characteriſtics were promptitude for duty and love of ſubordination as well as cheerfulneſs to encounter every ſpecies of difficulty and danger.

THE Rangers of Putnam ſoon opened their way for a junction with the little handful of Regulars, who ſtill obſtinately maintained their ground. By his advice the whole ruſhed impetuouſly with ſhouts and huzzas into the ſwamp. The Savages fled on every ſide and were chaſed, with no inconſiderable loſs on their part, as long as the day-light laſted. On ours only one man was killed in the purſuit. His death was immediately revenged by that of the Indian who ſhot him. This Indian was one of the Runners—a choſen body of active young men, who are made uſe of not only to procure intelligence and convey tidings, but alſo to guard the rear on a retreat.

HERE it will not be unſeaſonable to mention ſome of the cuſtoms in war, peculiar to the aborigines, which, on the preſent as well as other occaſions, they put in practice. Whenever a retreating, eſpecially, a flying party had gained the ſummit of a riſing ground; they ſecreted one or two runners behind trees, copſes or buſhes to fire at the enemy upon their aſcending the hill. This commonly occaſioned the enemy to halt and form for battle. In the interim the runners uſed ſuch dexterity as to be rarely diſcovered, or if diſcovered, they vaniſhed behind the height and rejoined their brother-warriors, who, having thus ſtolen a diſtance, were oftentimes ſeen by their purſuers no more. Or if the purſuers were too eager they ſeldom failed to atone for their raſhneſs by falling into an ambuſcade. The Mohawks, who were afterwards much employed in ſcouts under the orders of Major Putnam, and who were perfectly verſed in all the wiles and ſtratagems of their countrymen, ſhewed him the mode of avoiding the evils of either alternative. In ſuſpicious thickets and at the borders of every conſiderable eminence, a momentary pauſe was made, while they, in different parts, penetrated or aſcended with a cautiouſneſs that cannot be eaſily deſcribed. They ſeemed all eye and ear. When they found no lurking miſchief, they would beckon with the hand and pronounce the word, "OW-"ISH," with a long labial hiſſing, the *O* being almoſt quieſcent. This was ever the watchword for the main body to advance.

INDIANS, who went to war together and who for any reaſon found it neceſſary to ſeparate into different routes, always left two or three Runners at the place of ſeparation, to give timely notice to either party in caſe of purſuit.

IF a warrior chanced to ſtraggle and loſe

himſelf in the woods, or to be retarded by accident or wound; the party miſſing him would frequently, on their march, break down a buſh or a ſhrub and leave the top pointing in the direction they had gone, that the ſtraggler, when he ſhould behold it, might ſhape his courſe accordingly.

We come to the campaign when General Abercrombie took the command at Fort Edward. That General ordered Major Putnam, with ſixty men, to proceed by land to South Bay on Lake George, for the purpoſe of making diſcoveries and intercepting the enemy's parties. The latter, in complyance with theſe orders, poſted himſelf at Wood Creek, near its entrance into South Bay. On this bank, which forms a jutting precipice ten or twelve feet above the water, he erected a ſtone parapet thirty feet in length; and maſked it with young pine-trees, cut at a diſtance, and ſo artfully planted as to imitate the natural growth. From hence he ſent back fifteen of his men, who had fallen ſick. Diſtreſs for want of proviſions, occaſioned by the length of march and time ſpent on this temporary fortification, compelled him to deviate from a rule he had eſtabliſhed, never to permit a gun to be fired but at an enemy, while on a ſcout. He was now obliged himſelf to ſhoot a buck, which had jumped into the Creek, in order to eke out their ſcanty ſubſiſtence until the fourth day after the completion of the works. About ten o'clock that evening, one of the men on duty at the margin of the Bay informed him, that a fleet of bark canoes, filled with men, was ſteering towards the mouth of the creek. He immediately called in all his centinels and ordered every man to his poſt. A profound ſtillneſs reigned in the atmoſphere and the full moon ſhone with uncommon brightneſs. The creek, which the enemy entered, is about ſix rods wide, and the bank oppoſite to the parapet above twenty feet high. It was intended to permit the canoes in front to paſs—they had accordingly juſt paſſed, when a ſoldier accidentally ſtruck his firelock againſt a ſtone. The commanding officer in the van canoe heard the noiſe and repeated ſeveral times the Savage watch-word OWISH! Inſtantly the canoes huddled together, with their centre preciſely in front of the works, covering the creek, for a conſiderable diſtance, above and below. The officers appeared to be in deep conſultation and the fleet on the point of returning; when Major Putnam, who had ordered his men in the moſt peremptory manner, not to fire untill he ſhould ſet the example, gave the ſignal by diſcharging his piece.

They fired. Nothing could exceed the inextricable confusion and apparent consternation occasioned by this well concerted attack. But, at last, the enemy finding, from the unfrequency (though there was no absolute intermission) in the firing, that the number of our men must be small, resolved to land below and surround them. Putnam, apprehensive of this from the movement, sent Lieutenant Robert Durkee*, with twelve men, about thirty rods down the creek, who arrived in time to repulse the party which attempted to land. Another small detachment, under Lieutenant Parsons, was ordered up the creek to prevent any similar attempt. In the mean time, Major Putnam, kept up (through the whole night) an incessant and deadly fire on the main body of the enemy; without receiving any thing in return but shot void of effect, accompanied with dolorous groans, miserable shrieks and dismal savage yells. After

* As the name of the brave Durkee will occur no more in these sheets, I may be indulged in mentioning his melancholy fate. He survived this war, and was appointed a Captain in that war which terminated in the acknowledgement of our Independence. In 1778 he was wounded and taken prisoner by the Savages, at the battle of Wyoming on the Susquehannah. Having been condemned to be burnt, the Indians kept him in the flames with pitchforks, until he expired in the most excruciating torments.

day-break he was advifed that one part of the enemy had effected a landing confiderably below, and were rapidly advancing to cut off his retreat. Apprifed of the great fuperiority ftill oppofed to him, as well as of the fituation of his own foldiers, fome of whom were entirely deftitute of ammunition, and the reft reduced to one or two rounds per man, he commanded them to fwing their packs. By haftening the retreat, in good order, they had juft time to retire far enough up the creek to prevent being enclofed. During this long continued action, in which the Americans had flain at leaft five times their own number, only one Provincial and one Indian were wounded on their fide. Thefe unfortunate men had been fent off for camp in the night, with two men to affift them, and directions to proceed by Wood Creek as the fafeft, though not the fhorteft, route. But having taken a nearer way, they were purfued and overtaken by the Indians, who, from the blood on the leaves and bufhes, believed that they were on the trail of our whole party. The wounded, defpairing of mercy and unable to fly, infifted that the well foldiers fhould make their efcape, which, on a moment's deliberation, they effected. The Provincial, whofe thigh was broken by a ball, upon the approach of the Savages fired his piece and killed three of them; after which he was quickly hacked in pieces. The Indian, however, was ſaved alive. This man, Major Putnam ſaw, afterwards, in Canada. Where he likewiſe learned that his enemy in the re-encounter at Wood Creek conſiſted of five hundred French and Indians, under the command of the celebrated partizan Molang, and that no party, ſince the war, had ſuffered ſo ſeverely, as more than one half of thoſe who went out never returned.

OUR brave little company, reduced to forty in number, had proceeded along the bank of the creek about an hour's march, when Major Putnam, being in front, was fired upon by a party juſt at hand. He, rightly appreciating the advantage often obtained by aſſuming a bold countenance on a critical occaſion, in a ſtentorophonic tone ordered his men to ruſh on the enemy and promiſed that they ſhould ſoon give a good account of them. It proved to be a ſcout of Provincials, who conceived they were firing upon the French; but the Commanding Officer, knowing Putnam's voice, cried out "that they were all "friends."—Upon this the Major told him abruptly, "that friends or enemies, they all "deſerved to be hanged for not killing more "when they had ſo fair a ſhot." In fact, but one man was mortally wounded. While these things were tranſacted, a faithful ſoldier, whoſe ammunition had been early exhauſted, made his way to the Fort and gave ſuch information, that General Lyman was detached with five hundred men to cover the retreat. Major Putnam met them at only twelve miles diſtance from the Fort, to which they returned the next day.

In the winter of 1757, when Colonel Haviland was Commandant of Fort Edward, the barracks adjoining to the north-weſt baſtion took fire. They extended within twelve feet of the Magazine, which contained three hundred barrels of powder. On its firſt diſcovery, the fire raged with great violence. The Commandant endeavored, in vain, by diſcharging ſome pieces of heavy artillery againſt the ſupporters of this flight of barracks, to level them with the ground. Putnam arrived from the Iſland where he was ſtationed, at the moment when the blaze approached that end which was contiguous to the Magazine. Inſtantly a vigorous attempt was made to extinguiſh the conflagration. A way was opened by a poſtern gate to the river, and the ſoldiers were employed in bringing water; which he, having mounted on a ladder to the eves of the building, received and threw upon the flame. It continued, notwithftanding their utmoft efforts, to gain upon them. He ftood, enveloped in fmoke, fo near the fheet of fire, that a pair of thick blanket mittens were burnt entirely from his hands—he was fupplied with another pair dipt in water. Colonel Haviland fearing that he would perifh in the flames, called to him to come down. But he entreated that he might be fuffered to remain, fince deftruction muft inevitably enfue if their exertions fhould be remitted. The gallant Commandant not lefs aftonifhed than charmed at the boldnefs of his conduct, forbade any more effects to be carried out of the Fort, animated the men to redoubled diligence, and exclaimed "if we "muft be blown up, we will go all together." At laft, when the barracks were feen to be tumbling, Putnam defcended, placed himfelf at the interval, and continued from an inceffant rotation of replenifhed buckets to pour water upon the Magazine. The outfide planks were already confumed by the proximity of the fire; and as only one thicknefs of timber intervened, the trepidation now became general and extreme. Putnam, ftill undaunted, covered with a cloud of cinders and fcorched with the intenfity of the heat, maintained his pofition until the fire fubfided and the danger was wholly over. He had contended for one hour and an half with that terrible element. His legs, his thighs, his arms and his face were bliſtered; and when he pulled off his ſecond pair of mittens the ſkin from his hands and fingers followed them. It was a month before he recovered. The Commandant, to whom his merits had before endeared him, could not ſtifle the emotions of gratitude, due to the man who had been ſo inſtrumental in preſerving the Magazine, the Fort and the Garriſon.

THE repulſe before Ticonderoga took place in 1758. General Abercrombie, the Britiſh Commander in Chief in America, conducted the expedition. His army, which amounted to nearly ſixteen thouſand Regulars and Provincials, was amply ſupplied with Artillery and military Stores. This well-appointed corps paſſed over Lake George, and landed, without oppoſition, at the point of deſtination. The troops advanced in columns. Lord Howe having Major Putnam with him, was in front of the center. A body of about five hundred men (the advance or pickets of the French army) which had fled at firſt, began to ſkirmiſh with our left. "Putnam," ſaid Lord Howe, "what means that firing?" "I know not, but with your Lordſhip's leave "will ſee," replied the former. "I will ac-

" company you," rejoined the gallant young Nobleman. In vain did Major Putnam attempt to diffuade him by faying—" My " Lord, if I am killed, the lofs of my life " will be of little confequence, but the pre- " fervation of your's is of infinite importance " to this army." The only anfwer was, " Putnam, your life is as dear to you as mine " is to me; I am determined to go." One hundred of the van, under Major Putnam, filed off with Lord Howe. They foon met the left flank of the enemy's advance, by whofe firft fire his Lordfhip fell.—It was a lofs indeed; and particularly felt in the operations which occurred three days afterwards. His manners and his virtues, had made him the idol of the army. From his firft arrival in America, he had accommodated* himfelf and his regiment to the peculiar nature of the fervice. Exemplary to the officer, a friend of the foldier, the model of difcipline, he had not failed to encounter every hardfhip and hazard. Nothing could be more calculated to infpire men with the rafh animation of rage, or to temper it with the cool perfeverance of revenge, than the fight

* He cut his hair fhort and induced the Regiment to follow the example. He fafhioned their cloathing for the activity of fervice, and divefted himfelf and them of every article of fuperfluous baggage.

of ſuch a hero, ſo beloved, fallen in his country's cauſe. It had the effect. Putnam's party, having cut their way obliquely through the enemy's ranks, and having been joined by Captain D'Ell with twenty men, together with ſome other ſmall parties, charged them ſo furiouſly in rear, that nearly three hundred were killed on the ſpot and one hundred and forty-eight made priſoners. In the mean time, from the unſkillfulneſs of the guides, ſome of our columns were bewildered. The left wing, ſeeing Putnam's party in their front, advancing over the dead bodies towards them, commenced a briſk and heavy fire, which killed a Serjeant and ſeveral privates. Nor could they, by ſounds or ſigns, be convinced of their miſtake, until Major Putnam, preferring (if Heaven had thus ordained it) the loſs of his own life to the loſs of the lives of his brave aſſociates, ran through the midſt of the flying balls and prevented the impending cataſtrophe.

The tender feelings, which Major Putnam poſſeſſed, taught him to reſpect an unfortunate foe and to ſtrive by every lenient art in his power to alleviate the miſeries of war. For this purpoſe he remained on the field, until it began to grow dark, employed in collecting ſuch of the enemy as were left wounded to one place; he gave them all the liquor and little refreshments which he could procure; he furnished to each of them a blanket; he put three blankets under a French Serjeant who was badly wounded through the body, and placed him in an easy posture by the side of a tree—the poor fellow could only squeeze his hand with an expressive grasp. "Ah," said Major Putnam, "depend upon "it, my brave Soldier, you shall be brought "to the camp as soon as possible, and the "same care shall be taken of you as if you "were my brother."—The next morning Major Rogers was sent to reconnoitre the field and to bring off the wounded prisoners—but finding the wounded unable to help themselves, in order to save trouble, he dispatched every one of them to the world of Spirits. Putnam's was not the only heart that bled: The Provincial and British Officers who became acquainted with the fact were struck with inexpressible horror.

Ticonderoga is surrounded on three sides by water, on the fourth, for some distance extends a dangerous morass, the remainder was then fortified with a line eight feet high and planted with artillery. For one hundred yards in front, the plain was covered with great trees, cut for the purpose of defence;

whoſe interwoven and ſharpened branches projected outwards. Notwitſtanding theſe impediments, the Engineer, who had been employed to reconnoitre, reported, as his opinion, that the works might be carried with muſquetry. The difficulty and delay of dragging the battering cannon, over grounds almoſt impracticable, induced the adoption of this fatal advice—to which, however, a rumour that the garriſon, already conſiſting of four or five thouſand men, was on the point of being augmented with three thouſand more, probably contributed. The attack was as ſpirited in execution as ill-judged in deſign. The aſſailants, after having been for more than four hours expoſed to a moſt fatal fire, without having made any impreſſion by their reiterated and obſtinate proofs of valor, were ordered to retreat. Major Putnam, who had acted as an aid in bringing the Provincial regiments ſucceſſively to action, aſſiſted in preſerving order. It was ſaid that a great number of the enemy were ſhot in the head, every other part having been concealed behind their works. The loſs on our ſide was upwards of two thouſand killed and wounded. Twenty-five hundred ſtands of arms were taken by the French. Our army, after ſuſtaining this havoc, retreated with ſuch extraordinary precipitation, that they regained their camp at the ſouthward of Lake George, the evening after the action.

THE ſucceſſes, in other parts of America, made amends for this defeat. Louiſbourg, after a vigorous ſiege, was reduced by the Generals Amherſt and Wolf; Frontenac, a poſt of importance on the communication between Lake Ontario and the St. Lawrence, ſurrendered to Colonel Bradſtreet; and Fort Du Queſne, ſituated at the confluence of the Monongahela with the Ohio (the poſſeſſion of which had kindled the flame of war, that now ſpread through the four quarters of the globe) was captured by General Forbes.

A few adventures, in which the public intereſts were little concerned, but which from their peculiarity appear worthy of being preſerved, happened before the concluſion of the year. As one day, Major Putnam chanced to lie, with a batteau and five men, on the eaſtern ſhore of the Hudſon, near the Rapids, contiguous to which Fort Miller ſtood; his men on the oppoſite bank gave him to underſtand that a large body of Savages were in his rear and would be upon him in a moment.—To ſtay and be ſacrificed—to attempt croſſing and be ſhot—or to go down the falls, with an almoſt abſolute certainty of being drowned; were the ſole alternatives, that preſented themſelves to his choice. So inſtantaneouſly was the latter adopted, that one man who had rambled a little from the party, was, of neceſſity, left, and fell a miſerable victim to ſavage barbarity. The Indians arrived on the ſhore ſoon enough to fire many balls on the batteau before it could be got under way. No ſooner had our batteau-men eſcaped, by favor of the rapidity of the current, beyond the reach of muſket ſhot; than death ſeemed only to have been avoided in one form, to be encountered in another, not leſs terrible. Prominent rocks, latent ſhelves, abſorbing eddies, and abrupt deſcents, for a quarter of a mile, afforded ſcarcely the ſmalleſt chance of eſcaping without a miracle. Putnam, truſting himſelf to a good Providence whoſe kindneſs he had often experienced, rather than to men, whoſe tendereſt mercies are cruelty, was now ſeen to place himſelf ſedately at the helm, and afford an aſtoniſhing ſpectacle of ſerenity: His companions, with a mixture of terror, admiration and wonder, ſaw him, inceſſantly changing the courſe, to avoid the jaws of ruin, that ſeemed expanded to ſwallow the whirling boat. Twice he turned it fairly round to ſhun the rifts of rocks. Amidſt theſe eddies in which there was the greateſt danger of its foundering, at one moment the fides were expofed to the fury of the waves; then the ftern, and next the bow glanced obliquely onward, with inconceivable velocity.—With not lefs amazement the Savages beheld him fometimes mounting the billows, then plunging abruptly down, at other times fkillfully veering from the rocks, and fhooting through the only narrow paffage; until, at laft, they viewed the boat fafely gliding on the fmooth furface of the ftream below. At this fight, it is afferted, that thefe rude fons of nature were affected with the fame kind of fuperftitious veneration, which the Europeans in the dark ages entertained for fome of their moft valorous champions. They deemed the man invulnerable, whom their balls (on his pufhing from fhore) would not touch; and whom they had feen fteering in fafety down the rapids that had never before been paffed. They conceived it would be an affront againft the *Great Spirit*, to attempt to kill this favored mortal with powder and ball, if they fhould ever fee and know him again.

In the month of Auguft, five hundred men were employed, under the orders of the Majors, Rogers and Putnam, to watch the motions of the enemy near Ticonderoga. At South Bay they feparated the party into two equal divifions, and Rogers took a pofition on Wood Creek twelve miles diftant from Putnam. Upon being, fome time afterwards, difcovered, they formed a re-union and concerted meafures for returning to Fort Edward. Their march through the woods, was *in three divifions by* FILES, the right commanded by Rogers, the left by Putnam and the centre by Captain D'Ell. The firft night they encamped on the banks of *Clear River*, about a mile from old Fort Ann, which had been formerly built by General Nicholfon. Next morning, Major Rogers and a Britifh officer, named Irwin, incautioufly fuffered themfelves, from a fpirit of falfe emulation, to be engaged in firing at a mark. Nothing could have been more repugnant to the military principles of Putnam than fuch conduct; or reprobated by him in more pointed terms. As foon as the heavy dew which had fallen the preceding night would permit, the detachment moved in one body, Putnam being in front, D'Ell in center and Rogers in the rear. The impervious growth of fhrubs and underbrufh that had fprung up, where the land had been partially cleared fome years before, occafioned this change in the order of march. At the moment of moving, the famous French partizan Molang, who had been fent with five hundred men to intercept our party, was not more than one mile and an half diſtant from them. Having heard the firing, he haſted to lay an ambuſcade preciſely in that part of the wood moſt favorable to his project. Major Putnam was juſt emerging from the thicket into the common foreſt, when the enemy roſe, and with diſcordant yells and whoops, commenced an attack upon the right of his diviſion. Surpriſed, but undiſmayed, Putnam halted, returned the fire and paſſed the word for the other diviſions to advance for his ſupport. D'Ell came. The action, though widely ſcattered and principally fought between man and man, ſoon grew general and intenſely warm. It would be as difficult as uſeleſs to deſcribe this irregular and ferocious mode of fighting. Rogers came not up: but, as he declared afterwards, formed a circular file between our party and Wood Creek to prevent their being taken in rear or enfiladed. Succeſsful as he commonly was, his conduct did not always paſs without unfavorable imputation. Notwithſtanding it was a current ſaying in the camp, "that Rogers "always *ſent*, but Putnam *led* his men to ac-"tion," yet, in juſtice, it ought to be remarked here, that the latter has never been known, in relating the ſtory of this day's diſaſter, to affix any ſtigma upon the conduct of the former.

Major Putnam, perceiving it would be impracticable to croſs the Creek, determined to maintain his ground. Inſpired by his example, the officers and men behaved with great bravery: ſometimes they fought aggregately in open view, and ſometimes individually under cover; taking aim from behind the bodies of trees and acting in a manner independent of each other. For himſelf, having diſcharged his fuzee ſeveral times, at length it miſſed fire, while the muzzle was preſſed aganſt the breaſt of a large and well proportioned Savage. This *warrior*, availing himſelf of the indefenſible attitude of his adverſary, with a tremendous war-whoop ſprang forward, with his lifted hatchet, and compelled him to ſurrender; and having diſarmed and bound him faſt to a tree, returned to the battle.

The intrepid Captains D'Ell and Harman, who now commanded, were forced to give ground for a little diſtance: the Savages, conceiving this to be the certain harbinger of victory, ruſhed impetuouſly on, with dreadful and redoubled cries. But our two partizans, collecting a handful of brave men, gave the purſuers ſo warm a reception as to oblige them, in turn, to retreat a little beyond the ſpot at which the action had commenced,

Here they made a ſtand. This change of ground occaſioned the tree to which Putnam was tied to be directly between the fire of the two parties. Human imagination can hardly figure to itſelf a more deplorable ſituation. The balls flew inceſſantly from either ſide, many ſtruck the tree, while ſome paſſed through the ſleeves and ſkirts of his coat. In this ſtate of jeopardy, unable to move his body, to ſtir his limbs or even to incline his head, he remained more than an hour. So equally balanced and ſo obſtinate was the fight! At one moment, while the battle ſwerved in favor of the enemy, a young Savage, choſe an odd way of diſcovering his humour. He found Putnam bound. He might have diſpatched him at a blow. But he loved better to excite the terrors of the priſoner, by hurling a tomahawk at his head —or rather it ſhould ſeem his object was to ſee how near he could throw it without touching him—the weapon ſtruck in the tree a number of times at a hair's breadth diſtance from the mark. When the Indian had finiſhed his amuſement, a French Bas-Officer (a much more inveterate ſavage by nature, though deſcended from ſo humane and poliſhed a nation) perceiving Putnam, came up to him, and, levelling a fuzee within a foot of his breaſt attempted to diſcharge it; it miſſed fire—ineffectually did the intended victim, solicit the treatment due to his situation, by repeating, that he was a prisoner of war. The degenerate Frenchman did not understand the language of honor or of nature: deaf to their voice and dead to sensibility, he violently and repeatedly pushed the muzzle of his gun against Putnam's ribs, and finally gave him a cruel blow on the jaw with the butt of his piece. After this dastardly deed he left him.

At length the active intrepidity of D'Ell and *Harman, seconded by the persevering valor of their followers, prevailed. They drove from the field the enemy, who left about ninety dead behind them. As they were retiring Putnam was untied by the Indian who had made him prisoner and whom he afterwards called master. Having been conducted for some distance from the place of action, he was stripped of his coat, vest, stockings and shoes; loaded with as many of the packs of the wounded as could be piled upon him; strongly pinioned, and his wrists tied as closely together as they could be pulled with a cord. After he had marched, through no pleasant paths, in this painful

* This worthy officer is still living at Marlborough, in the State of Massachusetts.

manner, for many a tedious mile; the party (who were exceſſively fatigued) halted to breathe. His hands were now immoderately ſwelled from the tightneſs of the ligature: and the pain had become intolerable. His feet were ſo much ſcratched that the blood dropped faſt from them. Exhauſted with bearing a burden above his ſtrength, and frantic with torments exquiſite beyond endurance; he entreated the Iriſh Interpreter to implore as the laſt and only grace he deſired of the Savages, that they would knock him on the head and take his ſcalp at once, or looſe his hands. A French officer, inſtantly interpoſing, ordered his hands to be unbound and ſome of the packs to be taken off. By this time the Indian who captured him and had been abſent with the wounded, coming up, gave him a pair of Mocaſons and expreſſed great indignation at the unworthy treatment his priſoner had ſuffered.

That Savage Chief again returned to the care of the wounded, and the Indians, about two hundred in number, went before the reſt of the party to the place where the whole were, that night, to encamp. They took with them Major Putnam, on whom (beſides innumerable other outrages) they had the barbarity to inflict a deep wound with a tomahawk, in the left cheek. His ſufferings were in this place to be conſummated. A ſcene of horror, infinitely greater than had ever met his eyes before, was now preparing. It was determined to roaſt him alive.—For this purpoſe they led him into a dark foreſt, ſtripped him naked, bound him to a tree and piled dry bruſh with other fuel, at a ſmall diſtance, in a circle round him. They accompanied their labors, as if for his funeral dirge, with ſcreams and ſounds inimitable but by ſavage voices. Then they ſet the piles on fire. A ſudden ſhower damped the riſing flame. Still they ſtrove to kindle it, until, at laſt, the blaze ran fiercely round the circle. Major Putnam ſoon began to feel the ſcorching heat. His hands were ſo tied that he could move his body. He often ſhifted ſides as the fire approached. This ſight, at the very idea of which all but Savages muſt ſhudder, afforded the higheſt diverſion to his inhuman tormentors, who demonſtrated the delirium of their joy by correſpondent yells, dances and geſticulations. He ſaw clearly that his final hour was inevitably come. He ſummoned all his reſolution and compoſed his mind, as far as the circumſtances could admit, to bid an eternal farewell to all he held moſt dear. To quit the world would ſcarcely have coſt a ſingle pang but for the idea of home, but for the remembrance of domeſtic endearments, of the affectionate partner of his ſoul, and of their beloved offspring. His thought was ultimately fixed on a happier ſtate of exiſtence, beyond the tortures he was beginning to endure. The bitterneſs of death, even of that death which is accompanied with the keeneſt agonies, was, in a manner, paſt—nature, with a feeble ſtruggle, was quitting its laſt hold on ſublunary things—when a French officer ruſhed through the crowd, opened a way by ſcattering the burning brands, and unbound the victim. It was Molang himſelf—to whom a Savage, unwilling to ſee another human ſacrifice immolated, had run and communicated the tidings. That Commandant ſpurned and ſeverely reprimanded the barbarians, whoſe nocturnal Powwas and helliſh Orgies he ſuddenly ended. Putnam did not want for feeling or gratitude. The French Commander, fearing to truſt him alone with them, remained until he could deliver him in ſafety into the hands of his maſter.

The Savage approached his priſoner kindly and ſeemed to treat him with particular affection. He offered him ſome hard biſcuit, but finding that he could not chew them, on account of the blow he had received from the Frenchman, this more humane Savage ſoaked ſome of the biſcuit in water and made him ſuck the pulp-like part. Determined, however, not to loſe his captive (the refreſhment being finiſhed) he took the mocaſons from his feet and tied them to one of his wriſts: then directing him to lie down on his back upon the bare ground, he ſtretched one arm to its full length, and bound it faſt to a young tree; the other arm, was extended and bound in the ſame manner—his legs were ſtretched apart and faſtened to two ſaplings. Then a number of tall, but ſlender poles were cut down; which, with ſome long buſhes, were laid acroſs his body from head to foot: on each ſide lay as many Indians as could conveniently find lodging, in order to prevent the poſſibility of his eſcape. In this diſagreeable and painful poſture he remained until morning. During this night, the longeſt and moſt dreary conceivable, our hero uſed to relate that he felt a ray of cheerfulneſs come caſually acroſs his mind, and could not even refrain from ſmiling, when he reflected on this ludicrous groupe for a painter, of which he himſelf was the principal figure.

The next day he was allowed his blanket and mocaſons, and permitted to march without carrying any pack, or receiving any inſult. To allay his extreme hunger, a little bear's meat was given, which he ſucked through his teeth. At night, the party arrived at Ticonderoga and the priſoner was placed under the care of a French guard. The Savages, who had been prevented from glutting their diabolical thirſt for blood, took every opportunity of manifeſting their malevolence for the diſappointment, by horrid grimaces and angry geſtures; but they were ſuffered no more to offer violence or perſonal indignity to him.

After having been examined by the Marquis de Montcalm, Major Putnam was conducted to Montreal by a French officer, who treated him with the greateſt indulgence and humanity.

At this place were ſeveral priſoners. Colonel Peter Schuyler, remarkable for his philanthropy, generoſity and friendſhip, was of the number. No ſooner had he heard of Major Putnam's arrival, than he went to the Interpreter's quarters and enquired, whether he had a Provincial Major in his cuſtody? He found Major Putnam in a comfortleſs condition—without coat, waiſtcoat or hoſe—the remnant of his clothing miſerably dirty and ragged—his beard long and ſqualid—his legs torn by thorns and briars—his face gaſhed with wounds, and ſwollen with bruiſes. Colonel Schuyler, irritated beyond all ſufferance at ſuch a ſight, could ſcarcely reſtrain his ſpeech within limits, conſiſtent with the prudence of a priſoner and the meekneſs of a chriſtian. Major Putnam was immediately treated according to his rank, cloathed in a decent manner, and ſupplied with money by that liberal and ſympathetic patron of the diſtreſſed.

The capture of Frontenac by General Bradſtreet afforded occaſion for an exchange of priſoners. Colonel Schuyler was comprehended in the cartel. A generous ſpirit can never be ſatisfied with impoſing taſks for its generoſity to accompliſh. Apprehenſive, if it ſhould be known that Putnam was a diſtinguiſhed partizan, his liberation might be retarded, and knowing that there were officers, who, from the length of their captivity, had a claim of priority to exchange; he had, by his happy addreſs, induced the Governor to offer, that whatever officer he might think proper to nominate, ſhould be included in the preſent cartel. With great politeneſs in manner, but ſeeming indifference as to object, he expreſſed his warmeſt acknowledgements to the Governor and ſaid: "There is "an old man here, who is a Provincial Ma-

" jor and wiſhes to be at home with his wife " and children. He can do no good here, " or any where elſe: I believe your Excel-" lency had better keep ſome of the young " men, who have no wife or children to care " for, and let the old fellow go home with " me." This juſtifiable fineſſe had the deſired effect.

At the houſe of Colonel Schuyler, Major Putnam became acquainted with Mrs. Howe, a fair captive, whoſe hiſtory would not be read without emotion if it could be written in the ſame affecting manner, in which I have often heard it told. She was ſtill young and handſome herſelf, though ſhe had two daughters of marriageable age. Diſtreſs, which had taken ſomewhat from the original redundancy of her bloom and added a ſoftening paleneſs to her cheeks, rendered her appearance the more engaging. Her face, that ſeemed to have been formed for the aſſemblage of dimples and ſmiles, was clouded with care. The natural ſweetneſs was not, however, ſoured by deſpondency and petulance; but chaſtened by humility and reſignation. This mild daughter of ſorrow looked as if ſhe had known the day of proſperity, when ſerenity and gladneſs of ſoul were the inmates of her boſom. That day was paſt, and the once lively features now aſſumed a tender melancholy, which witneſſed her irreparable loſs. She needed not the cuſtomary weeds of mourning or the fallacious pageantry of woe to prove her widowed ſtate. She was in that ſtage of affliction, when the exceſs is ſo far abated as to permit the ſubject to be drawn into converſation without opening the wound afreſh. It is then rather a ſource of pleaſure than pain to dwell upon the circumſtances in narration. Every thing conſpired to make her ſtory intereſting. Her firſt huſband had been killed and ſcalped by the Indians ſome years before. By an unexpected aſſault in 1756 upon Fort Dummer, where ſhe then happened to be preſent with Mr. Howe her ſecond huſband, the Savages carried the Fort, murdered the greater part of the garriſon, mangled in death her huſband and led her away with ſeven children into captivity. She was for ſome months kept with them: and during their rambles ſhe was frequently on the point of periſhing with hunger, and as often ſubjected to hardſhips ſeemingly intolerable to one of ſo delicate a frame. Some time after the career of her miſeries began, the Indians ſelected a couple of their young men to marry her daughters. The fright and diſguſt which the intelligence of this intention occaſioned to theſe poor young creatures added infinitely to the ſorrows and perplexities of their frantic mother. To prevent the hated connection all the activity of female reſource was called into exertion. She found an opportunity of conveying to the Governor a Petition that her daughters might be received into a convent for the ſake of ſecuring the ſalvation of their ſouls. Happily the pious fraud ſucceeded.

About the ſame time the Savages ſeparated and carried off her five other children into different tribes. She was ranſomed by an elderly French officer for four hundred livres. Of no avail were the cries of this tender mother—a mother deſolated by the loſs of her children, who were thus torn from her fond embraces and removed many hundred miles from each other, into the utmoſt receſſes of Canada. With them (could they have been kept together) ſhe would moſt willingly have wandered to the extremities of the world, and accepted as a deſirable portion the cruel lot of ſlavery for life. But ſhe was precluded from the ſweet hope of ever beholding them again. The inſufferable pang of parting and the idea of eternal ſeparation planted the arrows of deſpair deep in her ſoul. Though all the world was no better than a deſert, and all its inhabitants were then indifferent to her

—yet the lovelineſs of her appearance in ſorrow had awakened affections, which, in the aggravation of her troubles, were to become a new ſource of afflictions.

THE officer, who bought her of the Indians, had a ſon who alſo held a commiſſion and reſided with his father. During her continuance in the ſame houſe, at St. John's, the double attachment of the father and the ſon rendered her ſituation extremely diſtreſſing. It is true the calmneſs of age delighted to gaze reſpectfully on her beauty, but the impetuoſity of youth was fired to madneſs by the ſight of her charms. One day the ſon, whoſe attentions had been long laviſhed upon her in vain, finding her alone in a chamber, forcibly ſeized her hand and ſolemnly declared that he would now ſatiate the paſſion which ſhe had ſo long refuſed to indulge. She recurred to intreaties, ſtruggles and tears, thoſe prevalent female weapons, which the diſtraction of danger not leſs than the promptneſs of genius is wont to ſupply: while he, in the delirium of vexation and deſire, ſnatched a dagger and ſwore he would put an end to her life if ſhe perſiſted to ſtruggle. Mrs. Howe, aſſuming the dignity of conſcious virtue, told him it was what ſhe moſt ardently wiſhed, and begged him to plunge the poignard through her heart, ſince the mutual importunities and jealouſies of ſuch rivals had rendered her life, though innocent, more irkſome and inſupportable than death itſelf. Struck with a momentary compunction, he ſeemed to relent and to relax his hold—and ſhe, availing herſelf of his irreſolution or abſence of mind, eſcaped down the ſtairs. In her diſordered ſtate, ſhe told the whole tranſaction to his father: who directed her in future to ſleep in a ſmall bed at the foot of that in which his wife lodged. The affair ſoon reached the Governor's ears, and the young officer was, ſhortly afterwards, ſent on a tour of duty to *Detroit.*

THIS gave her a ſhort reſpite; but ſhe dreaded his return and the humiliating inſults for which ſhe might be reſerved. Her children, too, were ever preſent to her melancholy mind. A ſtranger, a widow, a captive, ſhe knew not where to apply for relief. She had heard of the name of Schuyler—ſhe was yet to learn that it was only another appellation for the friend of ſuffering humanity. As that excellent man was on his way from Quebec to the Jerſeys, under a parole for a limited time, ſhe came with feeble and trembling ſteps to him. The ſame maternal paſſion, which, ſometimes, overcomes the timidity of nature in the birds when plundered of their callow neſtlings, emboldened her, notwithſtanding her native diffidence, to diſcloſe thoſe griefs which were ready to devour her in ſilence. While her delicate aſpect was heightened to a glowing bluſh, for fear of offending by an inexcuſeable importunity, or of tranſgreſſing the rules of propriety by repreſenting herſelf as being an object of admiration; ſhe told, with artleſs ſimplicity, all the ſtory of her woes. Colonel Schuyler from the moment became her protector and endeavored to procure her liberty. The perſon who purchaſed her from the Savages, unwilling to part with ſo fair a purchaſe, demanded a thouſand livres as her ranſom. But Colonel Schuyler, on his return to Quebec, obtained from the Governor an order, in conſequence of which Mrs. Howe was given up to him for four hundred livres—Nor did his active goodneſs reſt, until every one of her five ſons was reſtored to her.

Business having made it neceſſary that Colonel Schuyler ſhould precede the priſoners who were exchanged, he recommended the fair captive to the protection of his friend Putnam. She had juſt recovered from the meazles when the party was preparing to ſet off for New-England. By this time the young French officer had returned, with his paſſion rather encreaſed than abated by abſence. He purſued her wheresoever ſhe went, and, although he could make no advances in her affection, he ſeemed reſolved by perſeverance to carry his point. Mrs. Howe terrified by his treatment was obliged to keep conſtantly near Major Putnam, who informed the young officer that he ſhould protect that lady at the riſque of his life. However, this amorous and raſh lover, in whoſe boiling veins ſuch an agitation was excited, that while he was ſpeaking of her the * blood would frequently guſh from his noſtrils, followed the priſoners to Lake Champlain, and when the boat in which the fair captive was embarked had puſhed from the ſhore, he jumped into the Lake and ſwam after her until it rowed out of ſight. Whether he periſhed in this diſtracted ſtate of mind or returned to the ſhore is not known.

In the long march from captivity, through an inhoſpitable wilderneſs, encumbered with five ſmall children, ſhe ſuffered incredible hardſhips. Though endowed with maſcu-

* This phyſical effect, wonderful as it may appear, is ſo far from being a fictitious embelliſhment, that it can be proved by the moſt ſolemn teſtimony of more than one perſon ſtill living.

line fortitude, ſhe was truly feminine in ſtrength and muſt have fainted by the way, had it not been for the aſſiſtance of Major Putnam. There were a thouſand good offices which the helpleſſneſs of her condition demanded and which the gentleneſs of his nature delighted to perform. He aſſiſted in leading her little ones and in carrying them over the ſwampy grounds and runs of water, with which their courſe was frequently interſected. He mingled his own meſs with that of the widow and the fatherleſs, and aſſiſted them in ſupplying and preparing their proviſions. Upon arriving within the ſettlements they experienced a reciprocal regret at ſeparation, and were only conſoled by the expectation of ſoon mingling in the embraces of their former acquaintances and deareſt connections.

After the conqueſt of Canada in 1760, ſhe made a journey to Quebec in order to bring back her two daughters whom ſhe had left in a convent. She found one of them married to a French officer. The other, having contracted a great fondneſs for the religious ſiſterhood, with reluctance conſented to leave them and return.

A few years previous to the war between

Great Britain and America, a queſtion of ſome conſequence aroſe reſpecting the title of the lands in Hinſdale (the town in which Mrs. Howe reſided) inſomuch that it was deemed expedient, that an Agent ſhould be ſent to England to advocate the claim of the town. It may be mentioned as a proof of the acknowledged ſuperiority of the underſtanding and addreſs of this gentlewoman, that ſhe was univerſally deſignated for the miſſion. But the diſpute was fortunately accommodated to the ſatisfaction of the people, without their being obliged to make uſe of her talents.

We now arrive at the period, when the prowefs of Britain, victorious, alike by ſea and by land, in the new and in the old world, had elevated that name to the zenith of national glory. The conqueſt of Quebec, opened the way for the total reduction of Canada. On the ſide of the Lakes, Amherſt having captured the poſts of Ticonderoga and Crown Point, applied himſelf to ſtrengthen the latter. Putnam, who had been raiſed to the rank of a Lieutenant Colonel and preſent at theſe operations, was employed the remainder of this and ſome part of the ſucceeding ſeaſon in ſuperintending the parties, which were detached to procure timber and other materials for the fortification.

In 1760 General Amherst, a sagacious, humane and experienced commander, planned the termination of the war in Canada, by a bloodless conquest. For this purpose, three armies were destined to co-operate by different routes against Montreal, the only remaining place of strength the enemy held in that country. The Corps formerly commanded by General Wolf, now by General Murray, was ordered to ascend the river St. Lawrence; another (under Col. Haviland) to penetrate by the Isle aux Noix; and the third, consisting of about ten thousand men, commanded by the General himself, after passing up the Mohawk river and taking its course by the lake Ontario, was to form a junction by falling down the St. Lawrence. In this progress, more than one occasion presented itself to manifest the intrepidity and soldiership of Lieutenant Colonel Putman. Two armed vessels obstructed the passage and prevented the attack on Oswegatchie. Putnam, with 1000 men, in 50 batteaux, undertook to board them. This dauntless officer, ever sparing of the blood of others, as prodigal of his own, to accomplish it with the less loss, put himself (with a chosen crew, a beetle and wedges) in the van with a design to wedge the rudders, so that the vessels should not be able to turn their broadsides or perform any other manœuvre. All the men in his little fleet were ordered to ſtrip to their waiſtcoats and advance at the ſame time. He promiſed, if he lived, to join and ſhew them the way up the ſides. Animated by ſo daring an example, they moved ſwiftly, in profound ſtilneſs, as to certain victory or death. The people on board the ſhips, beholding the good countenance with which they approached, ran one of the veſſels on ſhore and ſtruck the colours of the other. Had it not been for the daſtardly conduct of the ſhip's company in the latter, who compelled the Captain to haul down his enſign, he would have given the aſſailants a bloody reception. For the veſſels were well provided with ſpears, nettings and every cuſtomary inſtrument of annoyance as well as defence.

It now remained to attack the fortreſs, which ſtood on an Iſland and ſeemed to have been rendered inacceſſible by an high abbatis of black-aſh, that every where projected over the water. Lieutenant Colonel Putnam propoſed a mode of attack and offered his ſervices to carry it into effect. The General approved the propoſal. Our partizan, accordingly, cauſed a ſufficient number of boats to be fitted for the enterprize. The ſides of each boat were ſurrounded with faſcines (musquet proof) which covered the men compleatly. A wide plank, twenty feet in length, was then fitted to every boat in such manner, by having an angular piece sawed from one extremity, that when fastened by ropes on both sides of the bow, it might be raised or lowered at pleasure. The design was that the plank should be held erect, while the oarsmen forced the bow with their utmost exertion against the abatis; and that, afterwards being dropped on the pointed brush, it should serve as a kind of bridge to assist the men in passing over them. Lieutenant Col. Putnam, having made his dispositions to attempt the escalade in many places at the same moment, advanced with his boats in admirable order. The garrison, perceiving these extraordinary and unexpected machines, waited not the assault, but capitulated. Lieutenant Colonel Putnam was particularly honored by General Amherst, for his ingenuity in this invention, and promptitude in its execution. The three armies arrived at Montreal, within two days of each other; and the conquest of Canada became compleat, without the loss of a single drop of blood.

At no great distance from Montreal stands the Savage village, called Cochnawaga. Here our partizan found the Indian Chief, who had formerly made him prifoner. That Indian was highly delighted to fee his old acquaintance, whom he entertained in his own well-built ftone houfe, with great friendfhip and hofpitality; while his gueft did not difcover lefs fatisfaction in an opportunity of fhaking the brave Savage by the hand and proffering him protection in this reverfe of his military fortunes.

When the belligerent powers were confiderably exhaufted, a rupture took place between Great Britain and Spain in the month of January 1762, and an expedition was formed that campaign, under Lord Albermarle, againft the Havannah. A body of Provincials, compofed of five hundred men from the Jerfeys, eight hundred from New-York and one thoufand from Connecticut, joined his Lordfhip. General Lyman, who raifed the regiment of one thoufand men in Connecticut, being the fenior officer, commanded the whole: of courfe the immediate command of his regiment devolved upon Lieutenant Colonel Putman. The fleet, that carried thefe troops, failed from New-York and arrived fafely on the coaft of Cuba. There a terrible ftorm arofe, and the tranfport, in which Lieutenant Colonel Putnam had embarked with five hundred men, was wrecked on a rift of craggy rocks. The weather was so tempestuous and the surf, which ran mountain-high, dashed with such violence against the ship, that the most experienced seamen expected it would soon part asunder. The rest of the fleet, so far from being able to afford assistance, with difficulty rode out the gale. In this deplorable situation, as the only expedient by which they could be saved, strict order was maintained and all those people, who best understood the use of tools, instantly employed in constructing rafts from spars, plank and whatever other materials could be procured. There happened to be on board a large quantity of strong cords (the same that are used in the whale fishery) which, being fastened to the rafts, after the first had with inconceivable hazard reached the shore, were of infinite service in preventing the others from driving out to sea, as also in dragging them athwart the billows to the beach: by which means, every man was finally saved. With the same presence of mind to take advantage of circumstances and the same precaution to prevent confusion, on similar occasions, how many valuable lives, prematurely lost, might have been preserved as blessings to their families, their friends, and their country. As soon as all were landed, Lieutenant Colonel

Putnam fortified his camp, that he might not be expofed to infult from the inhabitants of the neighbouring diftricts or from thofe of Carthagena, who were but twenty-four miles diftant. Here the party remained unmolefted feveral days, until the ftorm had fo much abated, as to permit the convoy to take them off. They foon joined the troops before the Havannah, who, having been feveral weeks in that unhealthy climate, already began to grow extremely * fickly. The opportune arrival of the Provincial reinforcement, in perfect health, contributed not a little to forward the works and haften the reduction of that important place. But the Provincials fuffered fo miferably by ficknefs, afterwards, that very few ever returned to their native land again.

Although a general peace among the Eu-

* Colonel Haviland (an accomplifhed officer feveral times mentioned in thefe memoirs) who brought to America a regiment of one thoufand Irifh veterans, had but feventy men remaining alive when he left the Havan. Colonel Haviland, during this fiege, having once with his regiment engaged and routed five hundred Spaniards, met Colonel Putnam on his return and faid—"Putnam, give me a pinch of fnuff." "I never carry any," returned Putnam.——"I have always juft fuch luck," cried Haviland, "the rafcally Spaniards have fhot away my pocket, fnuff-box and all."

ropean powers was ratified in 1763, yet the ſavages on our weſtern frontiers ſtill continued their hoſtilities. After they had taken ſeveral poſts, General Bradſtreet was ſent in 1764 with an army againſt them. Colonel Putnam, then for the firſt time appointed to the command of a regiment, was on the expedition; as was the Indian Chief (whom I have ſeveral times had occaſion to mention as his capturer) at the head of one hundred Cochnawaga warriors. Before General Bradſtreet reached Detroit, which the ſavages inveſted, Captain D'Ell, the faithful friend and intrepid fellow-ſoldier of Colonel Putnam, had been ſlain in a deſperate ſally. He, having been detached with five hundred men in 1763 by General Amherſt, to raiſe the ſiege, found means of throwing the ſuccour into the fort. But the garriſon (commanded by Major Gladwine, a brave and ſenſible officer) had been ſo much weakened, by the lurking and inſidious mode of war practiced by the ſavages, that not a man could be ſpared to co-operate in an attack upon them. The commandant would even have diſſuaded Captain D'Ell from the attempt, on account of the great diſparity in numbers; but the latter, relying on the diſcipline and courage of his men, replied "God forbid that I "ſhould ever diſobey the orders of my Gen-

" eral," and immediately diſpoſed them for action. It was obſtinate and bloody. But the vaſtly ſuperior number of the ſavages enabled them to encloſe Captain D'Ell's party on every ſide, and compelled him finally to fight his way in retreat from one ſtone-houſe to another. Having halted to breathe a moment, he ſaw one of his braveſt ſergeants lying at a ſmall diſtance wounded through the thigh and wallowing in his blood. Whereupon he deſired ſome of the men to run and bring the ſergeant to the houſe, but they declined it. Then declaring " that he never " would leave ſo brave a ſoldier in the field, " to be tortured by the ſavages," he ran and endeavored to help him up—at the inſtant, a volley of ſhot dropped them both dead together. The party continued retreating from houſe to houſe until they regained the fort; where it was found the conflict had been ſo ſharp and laſted ſo long, that only fifty men remained alive of the five hundred who had ſallied.

Upon the arrival of General Bradſtreet, the Savages ſaw that all further efforts in arms would be vain, and, accordingly, after many fallacious propoſals for a peace, and frequent tergiverſations in the negotiation, they concluded a treaty, which ended the war in America.

Colonel Putnam, at the expiration of ten years from his firſt receiving a Commiſſion, after having ſeen as much ſervice, endured as many hardſhips, encountered as many dangers and acquired as many laurels as any officer of his rank, with great ſatisfaction, laid aſide his uniform and returned to his plough. The various and uncommon ſcenes of war in which he had acted a reſpectable part, his intercourſe with the world and intimacy with ſome of the firſt characters in the army, joined with occaſional reading, had not only brought into view whatever talents he poſſeſſed from nature, but, at the ſame time, had extended his knowledge and poliſhed his manners to a conſiderable degree. Not having become inflated with pride or forgetful of his old connections, he had the good fortune to poſſeſs entirely the good will of his fellow citizens. No character ſtood fairer in the public eye for integrity, bravery and patriotiſm. He was employed in ſeveral offices in his own town and not unfrequently elected to repreſent it in the General Aſſembly. The year after his return to private life, the minds of men were ſtrangely agitated, by an attempt of the Britiſh Parliament, to introduce the memorable Stamp Act in America. This germe of policy, whoſe growth was repreſſed by the moderate temperature in which it was kept by ſome adminiſtrations, did not fully diſcloſe its fruit until nearly eleven years afterwards. All the world knows how it then ripened into a civil war.

On the twenty-ſecond day of March 1765 the Stamp Act received the royal aſſent. It was to take place in America on the firſt day of November following. This innovation ſpread a ſudden and univerſal alarm. The political pulſe in the Provinces, from *Main* to *Georgia*, throbbed in ſympathy. The Aſſemblies in moſt of theſe colonies, that they might oppoſe it legally and in concert, appointed Delegates to confer together on the ſubject. This firſt Congreſs met, early in October, at New-York. They agreed upon a Declaration of Rights and Grievances of the Coloniſts; together with ſeparate Addreſſes to the King, Lords and Commons of Great Britain. In the mean time, the people had determined, in order to prevent the ſtamped paper from being diſtributed, that the Stamp Maſters ſhould not enter on the execution of their office. That appointment, in Connecticut, had been conferred upon Mr. Ingerſol, a very dignified, ſenſible and learned native of the colony; who, upon being ſolicited to reſign, did not, in the firſt inſtance, give a ſatisfactory anſwer. In conſequence of which, a great number of the ſubſtantial yeomanry, on horſeback, furniſhed with proviſions for themſelves, and provender for their horſes, aſſembled in the eaſtern counties and began their march for New-Haven to receive the reſignation of Mr. Ingerſol. A junction with another body was to have been formed in Branford. But having learned at Hartford, that Mr. Ingerſol would be in town the next day to claim protection from the Aſſembly, they took quarters there and kept out patroles during the whole night, to prevent his arrival without their knowledge. The ſucceeding morning they reſumed their march and met Mr. Ingerſol in Wethersfield. They told him their buſineſs, and he, after ſome little heſitation, mounted on a round table and read his reſignation*.

* The curious may be pleaſed to know that the Reſignation was expreſſed in theſe explicit terms:

Wethersfield, September 9th, 1765.

" I do hereby promiſe, that I never will receive any " ſtamped papers which may arrive from Europe, in " conſequence of an Act lately paſſed in the Parliament " of Great Britain; nor officiate as Stamp Maſter or " Diſtributor of Stamps, within the colony of Connec- " ticut, either directly or indirectly. And I do hereby " notify to all the Inhabitants of his Majeſty's Colony of " Connecticut (notwithſtanding the ſaid office or truſt " has been committed to me) not to apply to me, ever " after, for any ſtamped paper; *hereby declaring that I*

That finished, the multitude desired him to cry out "liberty and property" three times; which he did, and was answered by three loud huzzas. He then dined with some of the principal men at a tavern, by whom he was treated with great politeness, and afterwards was escorted by about five hundred horse to Hartford: where he again read his resignation amidst the unbounded acclamations of the people. I have chosen to style this collection the *yeomanry*, the *multitude*, or the *people*, because I could not make use of the English word *mob* (which generally signifies a disorderly concurrence of the rabble) without conveying an erroneous idea. It is scarcely necessary to add, that the people, their object being effected, without offering disturbance, dispersed to their homes*.

" *do resign the said office*, and execute *these* PRESENTS
" of my own FREE WILL AND ACCORD, without any
" equivocation or mental reservation.

" In Witness whereof I have hereunto set my hand,

J. INGERSOL.

* To give a trait of the urbanity that prevailed, it may not be amiss to mention a jest that passed in the cavalcade to Hartford, and was received with the most perfect good humor. Mr. Ingersol, who, by chance rode a white horse, being asked " what he thought, to find " himself attended by such a retinue?"—replied, " that " he had now a clearer idea than ever he had before " conceived, of that passage in the Revelations, which " describes, '*Death on a pale horse and Hell following him.*'"

Colonel Putnam, who inſtigated the people to theſe meaſures, was prevented from attending by accident. But he was deputed ſoon after, with two other gentlemen, to wait on Governor Fitch on the ſame ſubject. The queſtions of the Governor and anſwers of Putnam will ſerve to indicate the ſpirit of the times. After ſome converſation, the Governor aſked, "what he ſhould do if the "ſtamped paper ſhould be ſent to him by "the King's authority?"—Putnam replied, "lock it up until we ſhall viſit you again."— "And what will you do then?" "We ſhall "expect you to give us the key of the room "in which it is depoſited; and, if you think "fit in order to ſcreen yourſelf from blame, "you may forewarn us upon our peril not to "enter the room."—"And what will you "do afterwards?"—"Send it ſafely back "again."—"But what if I ſhould refuſe ad- "miſſion?"—"In ſuch a caſe, your houſe "will be levelled with the duſt in five mi- "nutes."—It was ſuppoſed that a report of this converſation was one reaſon why the ſtamped paper was never ſent from New-York to Connecticut.

Such unanimity in the Provincial Aſſemblies and deciſion in the yeomanry carried, beyond the Atlantic, a conviction of the inexpediency of attempting to enforce the new Revenue Syſtem. The Stamp Act being repealed and the apprehenſions in a meaſure quieted: Colonel Putnam continued to labor with his own hands, at farming, without interruption, except, (for a little time) by the loſs of the firſt joint of his right thumb from one accident, and the compound fracture of his right thigh from another—that thigh, being rendered nearly an inch ſhorter than the left, occaſioned him ever after to limp in his walk.

THE Provincial Officers and Soldiers from Connecticut, who ſurvived the conqueſt of the Havannah, appointed General Lyman to receive the remainder of their prize money in England. A company, compoſed partly of military and partly of other gentlemen, whoſe object was to obtain from the Crown a grant of Land on the Miſſiſippi, alſo committed to him the negociation of their affairs. When ſeveral years had elapſed in applications, a Grant of Land was obtained. In 1770 General Lyman, with Colonel Putnam and two or three others went to explore the ſituation. After a tedious voyage and a laborious paſſage up the Miſſiſippi, they accompliſhed their buſineſs.

General Lyman came back to Connecticut with the Explorers, but ſoon returned to the Natchez: there formed an Eſtabliſhment and laid his bones. Colonel Putnam placed ſome laborers with proviſions and farming utenſils upon his location, but the encreaſing troubles ſhortly after ruined the proſpect of deriving any advantage from that quarter.

In ſpeaking of the troubles that enſued, I not only omit to ſay any thing, on the obnoxious claim aſſerted in the Britiſh declaratory act, the continuation of the duty on tea, the attempt to obtrude that article upon the Americans, the abortion of this project, the Boſton Port Bill, the alteration of the charter of Maſſachuſetts, and other topics of univerſal notoriety; but even wave all diſcuſſion of irritations on the one part and ſupplications on the other, which preceded the war between Great-Britain and her colonies on this continent. It will ever be acknowledged by thoſe who were beſt acquainted with facts, and it ſhould be made known to poſterity, that the king of England had not, in his extenſive dominions, ſubjects more loyal, more dutiful or more zealous for his glory than the Americans; and that nothing ſhort of a melancholy perſuaſion, that the "meaſures which "for many years had been ſyſtematically

" pursued, by his ministers, were calculated " to subvert their constitutions," could have dissolved their powerful attachment to that kingdom, which they fondly called their *parent country.* Here, without digressing to develope the cause, or describe the progress, it may suffice to observe, the dispute now verged precipitately to an awful crisis. Most considerate men foresaw it would terminate in blood. But, rather than suffer the chains (which they believed in preparation) to be rivetted, they nobly determined to sacrifice their lives. In vain did they deprecate the infatuation of those transatlantic councils which drove them to deeds of desperation. Convinced of the rectitude of their cause, and doubtful of the issue, they felt the most painful solicitude for the fate of their country, on contemplating the superior strength of the nation with which it was to contend. America, thinly inhabited, under thirteen distinct colonial governments, could have little hope of success, but from the protection of providence and the unconquerable spirit of freedom which pervaded the mass of the people: it is true, since the peace, she had surprisingly encreased in wealth and population —but the resources of Britain almost exceeded credibility or conception. It is not wonderful then, that some good citizens, of weaker nerves, recoiled at the profpect: while others, who had been officers in the late war, or who had witneffed by travelling the force of Britain, flood aloof. All eyes were now turned to find the men, who, poffeffed of military experience, would dare, in the approaching hour of fevereft trial, to lead their undifciplined fellow-citizens to battle. For none were fo ftupid as not to comprehend that want of fuccefs would involve the leaders in the punifhment of rebellion. Putnam was among the firft and moft confpicuous who ftepped forth. Although the Americans had been, by many who wifhed their fubjugation, indifcreetly as indifcriminately ftigmatifed with the imputation of cowardice—he felt —he knew for himfelf, he was no coward; and from what he had feen and known, he believed that his countrymen, driven to the extremity of defending their rights by arms, would find no difficulty in wiping away the ungenerous afperfion. As he happened to be often at Bofton, he held many converfations on thefe fubjects with General Gage the Britifh Commander in Chief, Lord Piercy, Colonel Sheriff, Colonel Small and many officers with whom he had formerly ferved, who were now at the Head Quarters. Being often queftioned, "in cafe the difpute fhould pro- "ceed to hoftilities, what part he would really

" take?" He always anſwered, " with his " country, and that, let whatever might hap- " pen, he was prepared to abide the conſe- " quence." Being interrogated " whether " *he*, who had been a witneſs to the proweſs " and victories of the Britiſh fleets and armies, " did not think them equal to the conqueſt of a " country which was not the owner of a ſin- " gle Ship, Regiment or Magazine?" He rejoined that " he could only ſay juſtice " would be on our ſide and the event with " Providence: but that he had calculated, " if it required ſix years for the combined " forces of England and her Colonies to con- " quer ſuch a feeble country as Canada; it " would at leaſt, take a very long time for " England alone to overcome her own wide- " ly extended Colonies, which were much " ſtronger than Canada: That when men " fought for every thing dear, in what they " believed to be the moſt ſacred of all cauſ- " es, and in their own native land; they " would have great advantages over their " enemies, who were not in the ſame ſitua- " tion: and that, having taken into view " all circumſtances, for his own part, he ful- " ly believed that America would not be ſo " eaſily conquered by England as thoſe gen- " tlemen ſeemed to expect. Being once, in particular, aſked, " whether he did not ſeri-

" ously believe that a well appointed British
" army of five thousand veterans could march
" through the whole continent of America?"
He replied briskly, " no doubt, if they be-
" haved civilly and paid well for every thing
" they wanted"—" but"—after a moment's
pause added—" if they should attempt it in a
" hostile manner (though the American men
" were out of the question) the women, with
" their ladles and broomsticks, would knock
" them all on the head before they had got
" half way through." This was the tenor, our hero hath often told me, of these amicable interviews. And thus, (as it commonly happens in disputes, about future events, which depend on opinion) they parted without conviction: no more to meet in a friendly manner, until after the appeal should have been made to Heaven and the issue confirmed by the sword. In the mean time, to provide against the worst contingency, the militia in the several Colonies was sedulously trained; and those select companies, the flower of our youth, which were denominated minutemen, agreeably to the indication of their name, held themselves in readiness to march at a moment's warning.

At length the fatal day arrived, when hostilities commenced. General Gage, in the evening of the 18th of April 1775, detached from Boſton the Grenadiers and Light Infantry of the Army, commanded by Lieutenant Colonel Smith, to deſtroy ſome military and other ſtores depoſited by the Province at Concord. About ſunriſe the next morning the Detachment, on marching into Lexington, fired upon a company of militia who had juſt reaſſembled: for having been alarmed late at night with reports that the Regulars were advancing to demoliſh the ſtores, they collected on their parade, and were diſmiſſed with orders to reaſſemble at beat of drum. It is eſtabliſhed by the affidavits of more than thirty perſons who were preſent, that the firſt fire, which killed eight of the militia then beginning to diſperſe, was given by the Britiſh without provocation. The ſpark of war, thus kindled, ran with unexampled rapidity and raged with unwonted violence. To repel the aggreſſion, the people of the bordering towns ſpontaneouſly ruſhed to arms and poured their ſcattering ſhot from every convenient ſtation upon the Regulars; who, after marching to Concord and deſtroying the Magazine, would have found their retreat intercepted, had they not been reinforced by Lord Piercy with the battalion companies of three regiments and a body of marines. Notwithſtanding the junction they were hard pushed and pursued until they could find protection from their ships. Of the British two hundred and eighty-three were killed, wounded and taken. The Americans had thirty-nine killed, nineteen wounded and two made prisoners.

Nothing could exceed the celerity with which the intelligence flew every where, that blood had been shed by the British troops. The country, in motion, exhibited but one scene, of hurry, preparation and revenge. Putnam, who was ploughing when he heard the news, left his plough in the middle of the field, unyoked his team, and without waiting to change his cloaths, set off for the theatre of action. But finding the British retreated to Boston and invested by a sufficient force to watch their movements, he came back to Connecticut, levied a regiment (under authority of the Legislature) and speedily returned to Cambridge*. He was now promoted to be

* An article (void of foundation) mentioning an interview between General Gage and General Putnam appeared in the English Gazettes in these words: "General Gage viewing the American army with his "telescope, saw General Putnam in it, which surprised "him; and he contrived to get a message delivered to "him, that he wanted to speak to him. Putnam, with-"out any hesitation, waited upon him. General Gage "shewed him his fortifications, and advised him to lay

a Major General on the Provincial Staff, by his Colony: and in a little time confirmed by Congress in the same rank on the Continental Establishment. General Ward of Massachusetts, by common consent, commanded the whole: And the celebrated Doctor Warren was made a Major General.

Not long after this period, the British Commander in Chief found the means to convey a proposal, privately, to General Putnam, that, if he would relinquish the Rebel party, he might rely upon being made a Major General on the British Establishment and receiving a great pecuniary compensation for his services. General Putnam spurned at the offer:

"down his arms. General Putnam replied, he could "force his fortifications in half an hour, and advised "General Gage to go on board the ships with his troops."

The apprehension of an attack, is adduced with much more verisimilitude, in M'Fingal, as the reason why General Gage would not suffer the inhabitants to go from the town of Boston, after he had promised to grant permission:

"So Gage of late agreed, you know,
"To let the Boston people go:
"Yet when he saw, 'gainst troops that brav'd him,
"They were the only guards that sav'd him,
"Kept off that Satan of a Putnam,
"From breaking in to maul and mutt'n him;
"He'd too much wit such leagues t' observe;
"And shut them in again to starve."

M'Fingal. Canto 1st.

which, however, he thought prudent at that time to conceal from public notice.

It could ſcarcely have been expected, but by thoſe credulous patriots who were prone to believe whatever they ardently deſired, that officers aſſembled from colonies diſtinct in their manners and prejudices, ſelected from laborious occupations to command a heterogeneous crowd of their equals compelled to be Soldiers only by the ſpur of occaſion, ſhould long be able to preſerve harmony among themſelves and ſubordination among their followers. As the fact would be a phænomenon, the idea was treated with mirth and mockery by the friends to the Britiſh government. Yet this unſhapen embryo of a military Corps, compoſed of militia, minutemen, volunteers and levies; with a burleſque appearance of multiformity in arms, accoutrements, cloathing and conduct, at laſt, grew into a regular Army—an Army which, having vindicated the rights of human nature and eſtabliſhed the independence of a new Empire, merited and obtained the glorious diſtinction of the patriot Army—the patriot Army, whoſe praiſes for their fortitude in adverſity, bravery in battle, moderation in conqueſt, perſeverance in ſupporting the cruel extremities of hunger and nakedneſs without a murmur or ſigh, as well as for their magnanimity in retiring to civil life, at the moment of victory, with arms in their hands and without any juſt compenſation for their ſervices, will only ceaſe to be celebrated, when time ſhall exiſt no more.

Enthusiasm for the cauſe of liberty, ſubſtituted in the place of diſcipline, not only kept theſe troops together, but enabled them at once to perform the duties of a diſciplined army. Though the Commanding Officers from the four colonies of New-England were in a manner independent, they acted harmoniouſly in concert. The firſt attention had been prudently directed towards forming ſome little redoubts and entrenchments; for it was well known that lines, however ſlight or untenable were calculated to inſpire raw ſoldiers with a confidence in themſelves. The next care was to bring the live ſtock from the Iſlands in Boſton bay, in order to prevent the enemy (already ſurrounded by land) from making uſe of them for freſh proviſions. In the latter end of May, between two and three hundred men were ſent to drive off the ſtock from Hog and Noddle Iſlands, which are ſituated on the North-Eaſt ſide of Boſton harbour. Advantage having been taken of the ebb-tide, when the water is fordable between the main and Hog Iſland, as it is between that and Noddle Iſland, the deſign was effected. But a ſkirmiſh enſued in which ſome of the Marines, who had been ſtationed to guard them, were killed: and as the firing continued between the Britiſh water-craft and our party, a reinforcement of three hundred men, with two pieces of artillery, was ordered to join the latter. General Putnam took the command, and having himſelf gone down on the beach within converſing diſtance and *ineffectually* ordered the people on board an armed Schooner to ſtrike, he plied her with ſhot ſo furiouſly that the crew made their eſcape and the veſſel was burnt. An armed ſloop was likewiſe ſo much diſabled as to be towed off by the boats of the fleet. Thus ended this affair, in which ſeveral hundred ſheep and ſome cattle were removed from under the muzzles of the enemy's cannon, and our men accuſtomed to ſtand fire, by being for many hours expoſed to it without meeting with any loſs.

The Provincial Generals, having received advice that the Britiſh Commander in Chief deſigned to take poſſeſſion of the heights on the peninſula of Charles Town, detached a thouſand men in the night of the 16th of June, under the orders of General Warren, to entrench themſelves upon one of theſe eminences, named Bunker Hill. Though retarded by accidents from beginning the work until nearly midnight, yet, by dawn of day, they had conſtructed a redoubt about eight rods ſquare and commenced a breaſt-work from the left to the low grounds; which an inſufferable fire from the ſhipping, floating batteries and cannon on Cop's Hill, in Boſton, prevented them from compleating. At mid-day four battalions of foot, ten companies of Grenadiers, ten companies of Light Infantry, with a proportion of artillery, commanded by Maj. Gen. Howe, landed under a heavy cannonade from the ſhips and advanced in three lines to the attack. The Light infantry, being formed on their right, was directed to turn the left flank of the Americans: and the Grenadiers, ſupported by two Battalions, to ſtorm the redoubt in front. Meanwhile, on application, theſe troops were augmented by the 47th Regiment, the 1ſt Battalion of Marines, together with ſome companies of Light Infantry and Grenadiers, which formed an aggregate force of between two and three thouſand men. But ſo difficult was it to reinforce the Americans, by ſending detachments acroſs the Neck which was raked by the cannon of the ſhipping, that not more than fifteen hundred men were brought into action. Few inſtances can be produced in the annals of mankind where Soldiers, who had never before faced an enemy or heard the whiſtling of a ball, behaved with ſuch deliberate and perſevering valor. It was not until after the Grenadiers had been twice repulſed to their boats, General Warren ſlain, his troops exhauſted of their ammunition, their lines in a manner enfiladed by artillery, and the redoubt half filled with Britiſh Regulars, that the word was given to retire. In that forlorn condition, the ſpectacle was aſtoniſhing as new, to behold theſe undiſciplined men, moſt of them without bayonets, diſputing with the butt end of their muſquets againſt the Britiſh bayonet and receding in ſullen deſpair. Still the Light Infantry, on their left, would certainly have gained their rear and exterminated this gallant little corps, had not a body of four hundred Connecticut men, with the Captains Knoulton and Cheſter, after forming a temporary breaſt-work by pulling up one poſt and rail fence and putting it upon another, performed prodigies of bravery. They held the enemy at bay until the main body had relinquiſhed the heights and then retreated acroſs the neck with more regularity and leſs loſs than could have been expected. The Britiſh, who effected nothing but the deſtruction of Charles Town by a wanton conflagration, had more than one half of their whole number killed and wounded: the Americans only three hundred and fifty-five killed, wounded and miſſing. In this battle the preſence and example of General Putnam, who arrived with the reinforcement, were not leſs conſpicuous than uſeful. He did every thing that an intrepid and experienced officer could accompliſh. The enemy purſued to Winter Hill—Putnam made a ſtand and drove them back under cover of their ſhips.

THE premature death of Warren, one of the moſt illuſtrious patriots that ever bled in the cauſe of Freedom; the veteran appearance of Putnam, collected yet ardent in action; together with the aſtoniſhing ſcenery and intereſting groupe around Bunker Hill; rendered this a magnificent ſubject for the hiſtoric pencil. Accordingly Trumbull, formerly an Aid de Camp to General Waſhington, afterwards Deputy Adjutant General of the northern Army, now an artiſt of great celebrity in Europe, hath finiſhed this picture with that boldneſs of conception and thoſe touches of art which demonſtrates the maſter. Heightened in horror by the flames of a burning town and the ſmoke of conflicting armies, the principal ſcene, taken the moment when Warren fell, repreſents that hero in the agonies of death, a Grenadier on the point of bayonetting him and Colonel Small (to whom he was familiarly known) arresting the Soldier's arm: at the head of the British line Major Pitcairne is seen falling dead into the arms of his son: and not far distant General Putnam is placed at the rear of our retreating troops, in the light blue and scarlet uniform he wore that day, with his head uncovered, and his sword waving towards the enemy, as it were to stop their impetuous pursuit. In nearly the same attitude he is exhibited by Barlow in that excellent Poem the Vision of Columbus.

" There strides bold Putnam and from all the plains,
" Calls the tired host, the tardy rear sustains,
" And, mid the whizzing death's that fill the air,
" Waves back his sword and dares the foll'wing war."*

* The writer of this Essay had occasion of remarking to the Poet and the Painter, while they were three thousand miles distant from each other (at which distance they had formed and executed the plans of their respective productions) the similarity observable in their descriptions of General Putnam.. These *Chefs d'œuvres* are mentioned, not with a vain presumption of adding eclat or duration to works which have received the seal of immortality, but because they preserve in the sister arts the same illustrious action of our hero. I persuade myself I need not apologize for annexing the beautiful lines from the poem in question, on the death of General Warren.

After this action, the British strongly fortified themselves on the Peninsulas of Boston and Charles Town: while the Provincials remained posted in the circumjacent country in such manner as to form a blockade. In the beginning of July, General Washington, who had been constituted by Congress Commander in Chief of the American forces, arrived at Cambridge to take the command. Having formed the army into three grand divisions, consisting of about twelve Regiments each, he appointed Major General Ward to command the right Wing, Major General Lee the left Wing and Major General Putnam the reserve. General Putnam's alertness, in accelerating the construction of the necessary defences, was particularly noticed and highly approved by the Commander in Chief.

About the 20th of July, the Declaration of Congress, setting forth the reasons of their taking up arms, was proclaimed at the head of the several Divisions. It concluded with

" There, hapless Warren, thy cold earth was seen,
" There spring thy laurels in immortal green;
" Dearest of Chiefs, that ever press'd the plain,
" In Freedom's cause, with early honors, slain,
" Still dear in death, as when in fight you mov'd,
" By hosts applauded and by Heav'n approv'd;
" The faithful muse shall tell the world thy fame,
" And unborn realms resound th' immortal name."

these patriotic and noble sentiments. "In
" our own native land, in defence of the free-
" dom that is our birth right, and which we
" ever enjoyed until the late violation of it;
" for the protection of our property, acquir-
" ed solely by the honest industry of our
" forefathers and ourselves; against violence
" actually offered; we have taken up arms.
" We shall lay them down when hostilities
" shall cease on the part of the aggressors,
" and all danger of their being renewed shall
" be removed, and not before.

" With an humble confidence in the mer-
" cies of the supreme and impartial Judge
" and Ruler of the Universe, we most de-
" voutly implore his divine goodness to con-
" duct us happily through this great conflict,
" to dispose our adversaries to reconciliation
" on reasonable terms, and, thereby, to re-
" lieve the empire from the calamities of ci-
" vil war."—As soon as these memorable words were pronounced to General Putnam's Division, which he had ordered to be paraded on Prospect Hill, they shouted in three Huzzas a loud amen! Whereat (a cannon from the Fort being fired as a signal) the new *Standard*, lately sent from Connecticut, was suddenly seen to rise and unroll itself to the wind. On one side was inscribed in large letters of

Gold "AN APPEAL TO HEAVEN," and on the other were delineated the armorial bearings of Connecticut, which without supporters or crest, consist unostentatiously of *three Vines*: with this motto, "**Qui transtulit,* " *sustinet*;" alluding to the pious confidence our forefathers placed in the protection of Heaven, on those three allegorical Scions—KNOWLEDGE—LIBERTY—RELIGION—which they had been instrumental in transplanting to America.

THE strength of position on the enemy's part and want of ammunition on our's prevented operations of magnitude from being attempted. Such diligence was used in fortifying our camps and such precaution adopted to prevent surprize, as to ensure tranquillity to the troops during the winter. In the spring a position was taken, so menacing to the enemy as to cause them, on the 17th of March 1776, to abandon Boston: not without considerable precipitation and dereliction of royal stores.

As a part of the hostile fleet lingered for sometime in Nantasket road (about nine miles below Boston) General Washington

* Literally, "*He who transplanted will support them.*"

continued himſelf in Boſton, not only to ſee the coaſt entirely clear, but alſo to make many indiſpenſable arrangements. His Excellency, propoſing to leave Major General Ward with a few regiments, to finiſh the fortifications intended as a ſecurity againſt an attack by water, in the mean time diſpatched the greater part of the army to New-York, where it was moſt probable the enemy would make a deſcent. Upon the ſailing of a fleet with troops in the month of January, Major General Lee had been ſent to the defence of that city; who, after having cauſed ſome works to be laid out, proceeded to follow that fleet to South Carolina. The Commander in Chief was now exceedingly ſolicitous that theſe works ſhould be completed as ſoon as poſſible, and accordingly gave the following

" Orders and Inſtructions for Major General Putnam.

" As there are the beſt reaſons to believe
" that the enemy's fleet and army, which left
" Nantaſket road laſt Wedneſday evening,
" are bound to New-York to endeavor to
" poſſeſs that important poſt, and, if poſſi-
" ble, to ſecure the communication by Hud-
" ſon's River to Canada; it muſt be our

" care to prevent them from accompliſhing " their deſigns. To that end, I have de- " tached Brigadier General Heath with the " whole body of Rifle men and five Batta- " lions of the Continental Army, by the way " of Norwich in Connecticut, to New-York. " Theſe by an expreſs arrived yeſterday from " General Heath, I have reaſon to believe " are in New-York. Six more Battalions, " under General Sullivan, march this morn- " ing by the ſame route, and will, I hope, " arrive there in eight or ten days at fartheſt. " The reſt of the army will immediately fol- " low in Diviſions, leaving only a conveni- " ent ſpace between each diviſion, to prevent " confuſion and want of accommodation up- " on their march. You will no doubt make " the beſt diſpatch in getting to New-York. " Upon your arrival there you will aſſume " the command and immediately proceed in " continuing to execute the *plan* propoſed by " Major General Lee, for fortifying that ci- " ty and ſecuring the paſſes of the Eaſt and " North Rivers. If, upon conſultation with " the Brigadiers General and Engineers, any " alteration in that *plan* is thought neceſſa- " ry, you are at liberty to make it: cautiouſ- " ly avoiding to break in too much upon his " main deſign, unleſs where it may be ap- " parently neceſſary ſo to do, and that by the

" general voice and opinion of the gentle-
" men abovementioned.

" You will meet the Quarter Master General Colonel Mifflin, and *Commissary General at New-York. As these are both men of excellent talents in their different Departments, you will do well to give them all the authority and assistance they require: And should a Council of War be necessary, it is my direction they assist at it.

" Your *long Service and Experience* will better than my particular directions at this distance, point out to you the works most proper to be first raised; and your perseverance, activity and zeal will lead you (without my recommending it) to exert every *Nerve* to disappoint the enemy's designs.

" Devoutly praying that the POWER which has hitherto sustained the American Arms, may continue to bless them with the divine protection, I bid you—FAREWELL.

Given at Head Quarters, in Cambridge,
this 29th of March 1776.

GEO. WASHINGTON.

* Colonel Joseph Trumbull, eldest son to the Governor of that name.

INVESTED with theſe commands, General Putnam travelled by long and expeditious ſtages to New-York. His firſt precaution, upon his arrival, was to prevent diſturbance, or ſurpriſe in the night ſeaſon. With theſe objects in view, after poſting the neceſſary guards, he iſſued his * Orders. He inſtituted, likewiſe, other wholeſome regulations to meliorate the police of the troops and to preſerve the good agreement that ſubſiſted between them and the citizens.

NOTWITHSTANDING the war had now raged, in other parts, with unaccuſtomed ſeverity for nearly a year, yet the Britiſh ſhips at New-York (one of which had once fired upon the town to intimidate the inhabitants) found the means of being ſupplied with freſh water and proviſions. General Putnam re-

* General Orders.

"Head Quarters New-York April 5, 1776.

"The Soldiers are ſtrictly enjoined to retire to their barracks and quarters, at tattoo-beating, and to remain there until the reveille is beat.

"Neceſſity obliges the General to deſire the inhabitants of the city to obſerve the ſame rule, as no perſon will be permitted to paſs any centry, after this night, without the counterſign.

"The Inhabitants, whoſe buſineſs requires it, may know the counterſign by applying to any of the Brigade-Majors."

ſolved to adopt effectual meaſures for putting a period to this intercourſe and accordingly expreſſed his prohibition* in the moſt pointed terms.

Nearly at the ſame moment, a detachment of a thouſand Continentals was ſent to occupy Governor's Iſland, a Regiment to fortify Red Hook, and ſome companies of Riflemen to the Jerſey ſhore. Of two boats, (belonging to two armed veſſels) which attempted to take on board freſh water from the watering place on Staten-Iſland, one was

* PROHIBITION.

" Head Quarters, New-York, April 8, 1776.

" The General informs the inhabitants that it is become abſolutely neceſſary, that all communication between the miniſterial fleet and ſhore ſhould be immediately ſtopped ; for that purpoſe he has given poſitive orders, the ſhips ſhould no longer be furniſhed with proviſions. Any inhabitants or others, who ſhall be taken that have been on board (after the publiſhing this order) or near any of the ſhips or going on board will be conſidered as enemies and treated accordingly.

" All boats are to ſail from Beekman's ſlip. Captain James Alner is appointed Inſpector and will give permits to Oyſtermen. It is ordered and expected that none attempt going without a paſs."

Israel Putnam, Major General in in the Continental Army and Commander in Chief of the forces in New-York.

driven off (by the Riflemen) with two or three seamen killed in it; and the other captured with thirteen. A few days afterwards Captain Vandeput of the Asia man of war, the senior officer of the ships on this station, finding the intercouse with the shore interdicted, their limits contracted, and that no good purposes could be answered by remaining there, sailed, with all the armed vessels, out of the harbor. These arrangements and transactions, joined to an unremitting attention to the completion of the defences, gave full scope to the activity of General Putnam, until the arrival of General Washington, which happened about the middle of April.

The Commander in Chief, in his first public orders, "*complimented the Officers who* "*had successively commanded at New-York,* " and returned his thanks to them as well as " to the Officers and Soldiers under their " command, for the many works of defence " which had been so expeditiously erected: " at the same time he expressed an expecta- " tion that the same spirit of zeal for the ser- " vice, would continue to animate their fu- " ture conduct."—Putnam, who was then the only Major General with the main army, had still a chief agency in forwarding the fortifications; and, with the assistance of the

Brigadiers Spencer and Lord Sterling, in aſſigning to the different Corps their alarm Poſts.

Congress having intimated a deſire of conſulting with the Commander in Chief on the critical poſture of affairs, His Excellency repaired to Philadelphia accordingly, and was abſent from the twenty-firſt of May until the ſixth of June. General Putnam, who commanded in that interval, had it in charge to open all letters directed to General Waſhington *on public ſervice*, and, if important, after regulating his conduct by their contents, to forward them by expreſs; to expedite the works then erecting; to begin others which were ſpecified; to eſtabliſh ſignals for communicating an alarm; to guard againſt the poſſibility of ſurprize; to ſecure well the Powder-Magazine; to augment by every means in his power the quantity of Cartridges; and to ſend Brigadier General Lord Sterling to put the Poſts in the *Highlands* into a proper condition of defence. He had alſo *a private and confidential inſtruction* to afford whatever aid might be required by the Provincial Congreſs of New-York for apprehending certain of their diſaffected citizens: and as it would be moſt convenient to take the detachment for this ſervice from the troops on Long-Iſland, under command of Brigadier General Greene, it was recommended that this officer ſhould be adviſed of the plan, and that the execution ſhould be conducted with ſecrecy and celerity, as well as with decency and good order. In the records of the army are preſerved the daily Orders which were iſſued in the abſence of the Commander in Chief, who, on his return, was not only ſatisfied that the works had been proſecuted with all poſſible diſpatch, but alſo that the other duties had been properly diſcharged.

It was the latter end of June when the Britiſh fleet, which had been at Halifax waiting for reinforcements from Europe, began to arrive at New-York. To obſtruct its paſſage ſome marine preparations had been made. General Putnam, to whom the directions of the whale boats, fire rafts, flat-bottomed boats and armed veſſels was committed, afforded his patronage to a project for deſtroying the enemy's ſhipping by exploſion. A *Machine*, altogether different from any thing hitherto deviſed by the art of man, had been invented by Mr. David Buſhnell*, for *ſubma-*

* David Buſhnell, A. M. of Saybrook in Connecticut, invented ſeveral other machines for the annoyance of ſhipping; theſe from accidents, not militating againſt the philoſophical principles, on which their ſucceſs de-

rine navigation, which was found to anſwer the purpoſe perfectly of rowing horizontally at any given depth under water, and of riſing or ſinking at pleaſure. To *this Machine* (called the American Turtle) was attached *a Magazine of Powder*, which it was intended

pended, only partially ſucceeded. He deſtroyed a veſſel in the charge of Commodore Symmonds, whoſe report to the Admiral was publiſhed. One of his kegs alſo demoliſhed a veſſel near the Long-Iſland ſhore. About Chriſtmas 1777 he committed to the Delaware a number of Kegs, deſtined to fall among the Britiſh fleet at Philadelphia: but his ſquadron of Kegs, having been ſeparated and retarded by the ice, demoliſhed but a ſingle boat. This cataſtrophe, however, produced an alarm, unprecedented in its nature and degree; which has been ſo happily deſcribed in the ſubſequent Song by the Hon. Francis Hopkinſon, that the event it celebrates will not be forgotton ſo long as mankind ſhall continue to be delighted with works of humour and taſte:

The battle of the Kegs:—a Song.—Tune Moggy Lawder.

GALLANTS, attend, and hear a friend
Trill forth harmonious ditty:
Strange things I'll tell, which late befell
In Philadelphia city.

'Twas early day, as poets ſay,
Juſt when the ſun was riſing,
A ſoldier ſtood on log of wood,
And ſaw a ſight ſurpriſing.

As in a maze, he ſtood to gaze,
The truth can't be denied, Sir,

to be faſtened under the bottom of a ſhip with a driving ſcrew; in ſuch ſort that the ſame ſtroke which diſengaged it from the Machine ſhould put the internal clock-work

He ſpied a ſcore of Kegs or more,
Come floating down the tide, Sir.

A ſailor, too, in jerkin blue,
The ſtrange appearance viewing,
Firſt damn'd his eyes, in great ſurprize,
Then ſaid—" Some miſchief's brewing."

" Theſe Kegs now hold the rebels bold,
" Pack'd up like pickled herring:
" And they 're come down, t' attack the town,
" In this new way of ferry'ng."

The ſoldier flew; the ſailor too:
And, ſcar'd almoſt to death, Sir,
Wore out their ſhoes to ſpread the news;
And ran till out of breath, Sir.

Now up and down, throughout the town,
Moſt frantic ſcenes were acted:
And ſome ran here and ſome ran there,
Like men almoſt diſtracted.

Some fire cried, which ſome denied,
But ſaid the earth had quaked:
And girls and boys, with hideous noiſe,
Ran through the town half naked

Sir William ‖ he, ſnug as a flea,
Lay all this time a ſnoring:

‖ Sir William Howe.

in motion. This being done, the ordinary operation of a gun-lock (at the diſtance of half an hour, an hour, or any determinate time) would cauſe the powder to explode and leave the effects to the common laws of nature. The ſimplicity, yet combination diſcovered

Nor dreamt of harm, as he lay warm
 In bed with Mrs. L*r*ng.

Now in a fright, he ſtarts upright,
 Awak'd by ſuch a clatter:
He rubs both eyes; and boldly cries,
 "For God's ſake, what's the matter?"

At his bed-ſide, he then eſpied
 Sir Erſkine † at command, Sir,
Upon one foot, he had one boot,
 And t'other in his hand, Sir,

"Ariſe! ariſe!" Sir Erſkine cries:
 "The rebels—more's the pity—
"Without a boat, are all on float,
 "And rang'd before the city.

"The motly crew, in veſſels new,
 "With Satan for their guide, Sir,
"Pack'd up in bags, or wooden KEGS,
 "Come driving down the tide, Sir;

"Therefore prepare for bloody war:
 "Theſe KEGS muſt all be routed:
"Or ſurely we deſpiſ'd ſhall be,
 "And Britiſh courage doubted."

† Sir William Erſkine.

in the mechanism of this wonderful machine, were acknowledged by those skilled in Physicks, and particularly Hydraulics, to be not less ingenious than novel. The Inventor,

The Royal band now ready stand,
All rang'd in dread array, Sir,
With stomach's stout, to see it out,
And make a bloody day, Sir.

The cannons roar from shore to shore:
The small arms make a rattle.
Since wars began, I'm sure no man
E'er saw so strange a battle.

The rebel * vales, the rebel dales,
With rebel trees surrounded,
The distant woods, the hills and floods,
With rebel echoes sounded.

The fish below swam to and fro,
Attack'd from ev'ry quarter:
"Why sure," thought they, "the Dev'l's to pay
"'Mongst folks above the water."

The KEGS, 'tis said, though strongly made
Of rebel staves and hoops, Sir,
Could not oppose their pow'rful foes,
The conqu'ring British troops, Sir.

From morn to night, those men of might,
Display'd amazing courage;
And when the Sun was fairly down,
Retir'd to sup their porridge.

* The British officers were so fond of the word, *rebel*, that they often applied it most absurdly.

whoſe conſtitution was too feeble to permit him to perform the labour of rowing the Turtle, had taught his brother to manage it with perfect dexterity; but unfortunately his brother fell ſick of a fever juſt before the arrival of the fleet. Recourſe was therefore had to a Serjeant in the Connecticut troops; who, having received whatever inſtructions could be communicated to him in a ſhort time, went (too late in the night) with all the apparatus under the bottom of the Eagle a ſixty-four gun Ship on board of which the Britiſh Admiral Lord Howe commanded. In coming up, the ſcrew, that had been calculated to perforate the copper ſheathing, unluckily ſtruck againſt ſome iron plates, where the rudder is connected with the ſtern. This ac-

An hundred men, with each a pen,
Or more, upon my word, Sir,
It is moſt true, would be too few,
Their valour to record, Sir.

Such feats did they perform that day,
Upon thoſe wicked Kegs, Sir,
That years to come, if they get home,
They'll make their boaſts and brags, Sir.

Mr. Buſhnell, having been highly recommended for his talents by Preſident Stiles, General Parſons and ſome other gentlemen of Science, was appointed a Captain in the Corps of Sappers and Miners: in which capacity he continued to ſerve with that corps, until the concluſion of the war.

cident, added to the ſtrength of tide which prevailed and the want of adequate ſkill in the Serjeant, occaſioned ſuch delay that the dawn began to appear: whereupon he abandoned the Magazine to chance, and (after gaining a proper diſtance) for the ſake of expedition, rowed on the ſurface towards the town. General Putnam, who had been on the wharf anxiouſly expecting the reſult from the firſt glimmering of light, beheld the Machine near Governor's Iſland and ſent a whale-boat to bring it on ſhore. In about twenty minutes afterwards the Magazine exploded and blew a vaſt column of water to an amazing height in the air. As the whole buſineſs had been kept an inviolable ſecret, he was not a little diverted with the various conjectures, whether this ſtupendous noiſe was produced by a bomb, a meteor, a water-ſpout or an earthquake. Other operations of a moſt ſerious nature rapidly ſucceeded and prevented a repetition of the experiment.

On the twenty-ſecond of Auguſt the van of the Britiſh landed on Long-Iſland, and was ſoon followed by the whole army, except one Brigade of Heſſians, a ſmall body of Britiſh and ſome convaleſcents, left on Staten Iſland. Our troops on Long Iſland had been commanded during the ſummer by

General Greene, who was now ſick; and General Putnam took the command, but two days before the battle of Flatbuſh. The Inſtructions to him (pointing in the firſt place to deciſive expedients for ſuppreſſing the ſcattering, unmeaning and waſteful fire of our men) contained regulations for the ſervice of the guards, the Brigadiers and the Field Officers of the day; for the appointment and encouragement of proper ſcouts; as well as for keeping the men conſtantly at their poſts; for preventing the burning of buildings (except it ſhould be neceſſary for military purpoſes) and for preſerving private property from pillage and deſtruction. To theſe regulations were added, in a more diffuſe though not leſs ſpirited and profeſſional ſtyle, reflections on the diſtinction of an army from a mob; with exhortations for the Soldiers to conduct themſelves manfully in ſuch a cauſe, and for their Commander to oppoſe the enemy's approach with detachments of his beſt troops: while he ſhould endeavor to render their advance more difficult by conſtructing abattis, and to entrap their parties by forming ambuſcades. General Putnam was within the lines, when an engagement took place on the 27th, between the Britiſh army and our advanced Corps, in which we loſt about a thouſand men in killed and miſſing, with the Generals Sullivan and Lord Sterling made prisoners. But our men (though attacked on all sides) fought with great bravery; and the enemy's loss was not light.

The unfortunate battle of Long Island, the masterly retreat from thence and the actual passage of part of the hostile fleet in the East River above the Town, preluded the evacuation of New-York. A promotion of four Major's General and six Brigadiers had previously been made by Congress. After the retreat from Long Island the main army, consisting for the moment, of sixty Battalions (of which twenty were Continental, the residue Levies and Militia) was, conformably to the exigencies of the service, rather than to the rules of war, formed into fourteen Brigades. Major General Putnam commanded the right grand Division of five Brigades, the Majors General Spencer and Greene the center of six Brigades, and Major General Heath the left which was posted near Kingsbridge and composed of two Brigades. The whole never amounted to twenty thousand effective men; while the British and German forces under Sir William Howe exceeded twenty-two thousand: indeed the Minister had asserted in Parliament that they would consist of more than thirty thousand. Our two center Divisions, both commanded by General Spencer in the sickness of General Greene, moved towards Mount Washington, Harlem Heights and Horn's Hook, as soon as the final resolution was taken, in a Council of War, on the twelfth of September, to abandon the city. That event, thus circumstanced, took effect a few days after.

On Sunday the fifteenth the British, after sending three ships of war up the North River to Bloomingdale and keeping up, for some hours, a severe cannonade on our lines, from those already in the East River, landed in force at Turtle Bay—our new Levies commanded by a state Brigadier General, fled without making resistance. Two Brigades of General Putnam's Division, ordered to their support, notwithstanding the exertion of their Brigadiers, and of the Commander in Chief himself, who came up at the instant, conducted themselves in the same shameful manner. His Excellency then ordered the Heights of Harlem, a strong position, to be occupied. Thither the forces in the vicinity, as well as the fugitives, repaired. In the mean time General Putnam, with the remainder of his command and the ordinary outposts, was in the city. After having caused the Brigades to begin their retreat by the route of Bloomingdale, in order to avoid the enemy, who were then in the possession of the main road leading to Kingsbridge, he galloped to call off the pickets and guards. Having myself been a Volunteer in his Division and acting Adjutant to the last Regiment that left the city, I had frequent opportunities that day of beholding him, for the purpose of issuing orders and encouraging the troops, flying, on his horse covered with foam, wherever his presence was most necessary. Without his extraordinary exertions the guards must have been inevitably lost, and it is probable entire Corps would have been cut in pieces. When we were not far from Bloomingdale, an Aid de Camp came from him at full speed to inform, that a column of British Infantry was descending upon our right. Our rear was soon fired upon, and the Colonel of our regiment (whose order was just communicated for the front to file off to the left) was killed on the spót. With no other loss, we joined the army, after dark, on the Heights of Harlem.

Before our Brigades came in, we were given up for lost by all our friends. So critical indeed was our situation and so narrow the gap by which we escaped, that the instant we had paſſed, the enemy cloſed it by extending their line from river to river. Our men, who had been fifteen hours under arms, harraſſed by marching and countermarching in conſequence of inceſſant alarms, exhauſted as they were by heat and thirſt (for the day proved inſupportably hot and few or none had canteens, inſomuch that ſome died at the brooks where they drank) if attacked, could have made but feeble reſiſtance.

If we take into conſideration the debilitating ſickneſs which weakened almoſt all our troops, the hard duty by which they were worn down in conſtructing numberleſs defences, the continual want of reſt they had ſuffered (ſince the enemy landed) in guarding from nocturnal ſurprize, the deſpondency infuſed into their minds by an inſular ſituation and a conſciouſneſs of inferiority to the enemy in diſcipline, together with the diſadvantageous terms upon which, in their ſtate of ſeparation, they might have been forced to engage; it appears highly probable that day would have preſented an eaſy victory to the Britiſh. On the other ſide, the American Commander in Chief had wiſely countenanced an opinion, then univerſally credited, that our army was three times more numerous that it was in reality. It is not a ſubject for aſtoniſhment, that the Britiſh, ignorant of the exiſting circumſtances, impoſed upon as to the numbers by reports and recollecting what a few brave men, ſlightly entrenched, had performed at Bunker Hill, ſhould proceed with great circumſpection. For their reproaches, that the Rebels (as they affected to ſtyle us) loved digging better than fighting, and that they earthed themſelves in holes like foxes, but ill concealed at the bottom of their own hearts the profound impreſſion that action had made. Cheap and contemptible as we had once ſeemed in their eyes, it had taught them to hold us in ſome reſpect. This reſpect, in conjunction with a fixed belief that the enthuſiaſtic ſpirit of our oppoſition muſt ſoon ſubſide, and that the inexhauſtible reſources of Britain would ultimately triumph without leaving any thing to chance (not the avarice or treachery of the Britiſh General, as the factions of his own nation wiſhed to inſinuate)retarded their operation and afforded us leiſure to reſcue from annihilation the miſerable relics of an army, haſtening to diſſolution by the expiration of enliſtments, and the country itſelf from irretreivable ſubjugation. IN TRUTH WE ARE NOT LESS INDEBTED TO THE MATTOCK AT ONE PERIOD, THAN TO THE MUSQUET AT ANOTHER, FOR OUR POLITICAL SALVATION. It required great talents to determine when one or the other was moſt profitably to be employed. I am aware how faſhionable it has become to compare the American Commander in Chief, for the prudence diſplayed in thoſe dilatory and defenſive operations, ſo happily proſecuted in the early ſtages of the war, to the illuſtrious Roman, who acquired immortality in reſtoring the Commonwealth, *by delay*. Advantageous and flattering as the compariſon at firſt appears, it will be found on examination to ſtint the American to the ſmaller moiety of his merited fame. Did HE not in ſcenes of almoſt unparalleled activity diſcover ſpecimens of tranſcendent abilities, and might it not be proved to profeſſional men, that boldneſs in council, and rapidity in execution were, at leaſt, equally with prudent procraſtination, and the quality of not being compelled to action, attributes of his military genius? *This*, however, was an occaſion, apparent as preſſing, for attaining his object *by delay*. From that he had every thing to gain, nothing to loſe. Yet there were not wanting *Politicians*, AT THIS VERY TIME, who querulouſly blamed theſe *Fabian* meaſures and loudly clamoured, that the immenſe labour and expence beſtowed on the fortification of New-York had been thrown away; that, if we could not face the enemy *there* after ſo many preparations, we might as well relinquiſh the conteſt at once, for we could no where make a ſtand; and that, if General Waſhington, with an army of ſixty thouſand men, ſtrongly entrenched, declined fighting with Sir William Howe, who had little more than one third of that number, it was not to be expected he would find any other occaſion that might induce him to engage.—But General Waſhington, content to ſuffer a temporary ſacrifice of perſonal reputation for the ſake of ſecuring a permanent advantage to his country, and regardleſs of thoſe idle clamours for which he had furniſhed materials by making his countrymen, in order the more effectually to make his enemy, believe his force much greater than it actually was; inflexibly purſued his ſyſtem and glorioufly demonſtrated how poor and pitiful in the eſtimation of A GREAT MIND are the cenſorious ſtrictures of thoſe Novices in war and politics, who, with equal raſhneſs and impudence, preſume to decide dogmatically on the merit of plans they could neither originate or comprehend!—

That night our ſoldiers exceſſively fatigued by the ſultry march of the day, their cloaths wet by a ſevere ſhower of rain that ſucceeded towards the evening, their blood chilled by the cold wind that produced a ſudden change in the temperature of the air, and their hearts ſunk within them by the loſs of baggage, artillery, and works in which they had been taught to put great confidence, lay upon their arms, covered only by the clouds of an uncomfortable ſky. To retrieve our diſorded affairs and prevent the enemy from profiting by them, no exertion was relaxed, no vigilance remitted on the part of our higher officers. The Regiments which had been leaſt expoſed to fatigue that day, furniſhed the neceſſary piquets to ſecure the army from ſurprize. Thoſe, whoſe military lives had been ſhort and unpracticed, felt enough beſides laſſitude of body to diſquiet the tranquillity of their repoſe. Nor had thoſe, who were older in ſervice and of more experience, any ſubject for conſolation. The warmth of enthuſiaſm ſeemed to be extinguiſhed. The force of diſcipline had not ſufficiently occupied its place to give men a dependence upon each other. We were apparently about to reap the bitter fruits of that jealous policy, which ſome leading men (with the beſt motives) had ſown in our fœderal councils, when they cauſed the mode to be adopted, for carrying on the war by detachments of militia; from apprehenſion that an eſtabliſhed Continental army, after defending the country againſt foreign invaſion, might ſubvert its

M 2

liberties themſelves. Paradoxical as it will appear, it may be profitable to be known to poſterity, that, while our very exiſtence as an independent people was in queſtion, the patriotic jealouſy for the ſafety of our future *freedom* had been carried to ſuch a virtuous, but dangerous exceſs, as well nigh to preclude the attainment of our Independence. Happily that limited and hazardous ſyſtem ſoon gave room to one more enlightened and ſalutary. This may be attributed to the reiterated arguments, the open remonſtrances and the confidential communications of the Commander in Chief: who, though not apt to deſpair of the Republic, on this occaſion, expreſſed himſelf in terms of unuſual deſpondency. He declared in his letters that he found, to his utter aſtoniſhment and mortification, that no reliance could be placed on a great proportion of his preſent troops, and that, unleſs efficient meaſures for eſtabliſhing a permanent force ſhould be ſpeedily purſued, we had every reaſon to fear the final ruin of our cauſe.

Next morning ſeveral parties of the enemy appeared upon the plains in our front. On receiving this intelligence, General Waſhington rode quickly to the out poſts, for the purpoſe of preparing againſt an attack, if the enemy ſhould advance with that deſign. Lieutenant Colonel Knowlton's Rangers (a fine ſelection from the eaſtern Regiments), who had been ſkirmiſhing with an advanced party, came in and informed the General that a body of Britiſh were under cover of a ſmall eminence at no conſiderable diſtance. His Excellency, willing to raiſe our men from their dejection by the ſplender of ſome little ſucceſs, ordered Lieutenant Colonel Knowlton with his Rangers, and Major Leitch with three Companies of Weedon's Regiment of Virginians to gain their rear; while appearances ſhould be made of an attack in front. As ſoon as the enemy ſaw the party ſent to decoy them, they ran precipitately down the hill, took poſſeſſion of ſome fences and buſhes, and commenced a briſk firing at long ſhot. Unfortunately Knowlton and Leitch made their onſet rather in flank than in rear. The enemy changed their front and the ſkirmiſh, at once became cloſe and warm. Major *Leitch having received three balls through his ſide was ſoon borne from the field, and Colonel Knowlton (who had diſtinguiſhed himſelf ſo gallantly at the battle of Bunker-Hill) was mortally wounded immediately af-

* Major Leitch, after languiſhing ſome days, died of a locked jaw.

ter. Their men, however, undaunted by these disasters, stimulated with the thirst of revenge for the loss of their leaders, and conscious of acting under the eye of the Commander in Chief, maintained the conflict with uncommon spirit and perseverance. But the General, seeing them in need of support, advanced part of the Maryland Regiments of Griffith and Richardson, together with some detachments from such eastern Corps, as chanced to be most contiguous to the place of action. Our troops this day, without exception, behaved with the greatest intrepidity. So bravely did they repulse the British, that Sir William Howe moved his *Reserve* with two field pieces, a battalion of Hessian Grenadiers and a company of Chasseurs to succour his retreating troops. General Washington, not willing to draw on a general action, declined pressing the pursuit. In this engagement were the second and third Battalions of Light Infantry, the forty-second British Regiment and the German Chasseurs, of whom eight officers and upward of seventy privates were wounded, and our people buried nearly twenty who were left dead on the field. We had about forty wounded: our loss in killed, except of two valuable Officers, was very inconsiderable.

An * advantage, ſo trivial in itſelf, produced, in event, a ſurpriſing and almoſt incredible effect upon the whole army. Among the troops not engaged, who during the action were throwing earth from the new trenches, with an alacrity that indicated a determination to defend them, every viſage was ſeen to brighten, and to aſſume, inſtead of the gloom of deſpair, the glow of animation.

* A tranſcript from General Waſhington's Public Orders of the ſeventeenth, will, better than any other document that could be adduced, ſhew his ſentiment on the conduct of the two preceding days and how fervently he wiſhed to foſter the good diſpoſitions diſcovered on the laſt.

"ORDERS.

"Head Quarters, Harlem Heights, Sept. 17, 1776.

"Parole Leitch. Counterſign Virginia.

"The General moſt heartily thanks the troops commanded yeſterday by Major Leitch, who firſt advanced upon the enemy, and the others who ſo reſolutely ſupported them. The behaviour yeſterday was ſuch a contraſt to that of ſome of the troops the day before, as muſt ſhew what may be done where Officers and Soldiers will exert themſelves. Once more, therefore, the General calls upon Officers and Men, to act up to the noble cauſe in which they are engaged, and to ſupport the *honor* and *liberties* of their Country."

"The gallant and brave Colonel Knowlton, who would have been an honor to any Country, having fallen yeſterday while gloriouſly fighting; Captain Brown is to take the Command of the party lately led by Colonel Knowlton. Officers and men are to obey him accordingly."

This change, no leſs ſudden than happy, left little room to doubt that the men, who ran the day before at the ſight of an enemy, would now (to wipe away the ſtain of that diſgrace and to recover the confidence of their General) have conducted themſelves in a very different manner. Some alteration was made in the diſtribution of Corps to prevent the Britiſh from gaining either flank in the ſucceeding night. General Putnam, who commanded on the right, was directed in orders, in caſe the enemy ſhould attempt to force the paſs, to apply for a reinforcement to General Spencer, who commanded on the left.

General Putnam, who was too good a huſbandman himſelf not to have a reſpect for the labors and improvements of others, ſtrenuouſly ſeconded the views of the Commander in Chief in preventing the devaſtation of Farms and the violation of private property. For under pretext that the property in this quarter belonged to friends to the Britiſh government (as indeed it moſtly did) a ſpirit of rapine and licentiouſneſs began to prevail, which, unleſs repreſſed in the beginning, foreboded, beſides the ſubverſion of diſcipline, the diſgrace and defeat of our arms.

Our new defences now becoming ſo ſtrong

as not to admit insult with impunity, and Sir William Howe, not choosing to place too much at risque in attacking us in front, on the 12th day of October, leaving Lord Piercy with one Hessian and two British Brigades in his lines at Harlem to cover New-York, embarked with the main body of his army with an intention of landing at *Frog's Neck*, situated near the town of West Chester and little more than a league above the communication called King's bridge, which connects New-York Island with the main. There was nothing to oppose him; and he effected his debarkation by nine o'clock in the morning. The same policy of keeping our army as compact as possible; the same system of avoiding being forced to action; and the same precaution to prevent the interruption of supplies, reinforcements or retreat, that lately dictated the evacuation of New-York, now induced General Washington to move towards the strong grounds in the upper part of West Chester County.

About the same time, General Putnam was sent to the western side of the Hudson to provide against an irruption into the Jerseys, and soon after to Philadelphia to put that town into a posture of defence. Thither I attend him, without stopping to dilate on the ſubſequent incidents that might ſwell a folio, though here compreſſed to a ſingle paragraph: without attempting to give in detail the ſkillful retrograde movements of our Commander in Chief, who, after detaching a Garriſon for Fort Waſhington, by preoccupying with extemporaneous redoubts and entrenchments the ridges from *Mile-Square* to *White Plains*, and by folding one Brigade behind another in rear of thoſe ridges that run parallel with the *Sound*, brought off all his Artillery, Stores and Sick, in the face of a ſuperior foe: without commenting on the partial and equivocal battle fought near the laſt mentioned village, or the cauſe why the Britiſh, then in full force (for the laſt of the Heſſian Infantry and Britiſh Light-Horſe had juſt arrived) did not more ſeriouſly endeavor to induce a general engagement: without journalizing their military manœuvres in falling back to Kingſbridge, capturing Fort Waſhington, Fort Lee, and marching through the Jerſeys: without enumerating the inſtances of rapine, murder, luſt and devaſtation, that marked their progreſs, and filled our boſoms with horror and indignation: without deſcribing how a diviſion of our diſſolving army, with General Waſhington, was driven before them beyond the Delaware: without painting the naked and forlorn condition of theſe much enduring men, amidſt the rigors of an inclement ſeaſon:

and without even ſketching the conſternation that ſeized the States, at this perilous period, when General Lee (in leading from the North a ſmall reinforcement to our troops) was himſelf taken priſoner by ſurprize; when every thing ſeemed decidedly declining to the laſt extremity, and when every proſpect but ſerved to augment the depreſſion of deſpair—until the genius of one man, in one day, at a ſingle ſtroke, wreſted from the veteran Battalions of Britain and Germany the fruits acquired by the total operations of a ſucceſsful campaign, and reanimated the expiring hope of a whole nation, by the glorious enterprize at Trenton.

While the hoſtile forces, raſhly inflated with pride by a ſeries of uninterrupted ſucceſſes, and fondly dreaming that a period would ſoon be put to their labors by the completion of their conqueſts, had been purſuing the wretched remnants of a diſbanded army to the banks of the Delaware: General Putnam was diligently employed in fortifying Philadelphia, the capture of which appeared indubitably to be their principal object. Here, by authority and example, he ſtrove to conciliate contending factions, and to excite the citizens to uncommon efforts in defence of every thing intereſting to Freemen. His personal industry was unparallelled. His *Orders with respect to extinguishing accidental fires, advancing the public works, as well as in regard to other important objects were perfectly military and proper. But his health was, for a while, impaired by his unrelaxed exertions.

The Commander in Chief, having in spite of all obstacles made good his retreat over the Delaware, wrote to General Putnam (from his Camp above the Falls of Trenton, on the very day he recrossed the river to surprise the

* As a specimen the following is preserved:

"GENERAL ORDERS.

"Head Quarters, Philadelphia, Dec. 14, 1776.

"Colonel Griffin is appointed Adjutant General to the troops in and about this city. All Orders from the General, through him, either written or verbal, are to be strictly attended to and punctually obeyed.

"In case of an alarm of fire, the city guards and patroles are to suffer the inhabitants to pass unmolested at any hour of the night; and the good people of Philadelphia are earnestly requested and desired to give every assistance in their power, with engines and buckets, to extinguish the fire. And, as the Congress have ordered the City to be defended to the last extremity, the General hopes that no person will refuse to give every assistance possible to complete the Fortifications that are to be erected in and about the City.

ISRAEL PUTNAM."

Heſſians) expreſſing his ſatisfaction at the re-eſtabliſhment of that General's health, and informing that, if he had not himſelf been well convinced before of the enemy's intention to poſſeſs themſelves of Philadelphia, as ſoon as the froſt ſhould form ice ſtrong enough to tranſport them and their artillery acroſs the Delaware, he had now obtained an intercepted letter which placed the matter beyond a doubt. He added that, if the citizens of Philadelphia had any regard for the town, not a moment's time was to be loſt until it ſhould be put in the beſt poſſible poſture of defence: but, leaſt that ſhould not be done, he directed the removal of all public Stores, except proviſions neceſſary for immediate uſe, to places of greater ſecurity. He queried whether, if a party of Militia could be ſent from Philadelphia to ſupport thoſe in the Jerſeys about Mount Holly, it would not ſerve to ſave them from ſubmiſſion? At the ſame time, he ſignified (as his opinion) the expediency of ſending an active and influential Officer to inſpirit the people, to encourage them to aſſemble in arms, as well as to keep thoſe already in arms from diſbanding; and concluded by manifeſting a wiſh that Colonel Forman, whom he deſired to ſee for this purpoſe, might be employed on the ſervice.

The enemy had vainly as incautiously imagined that to overrun was to conquer. They had even carried their presumption on our extreme weakness and expected submission, so far as to attempt covering the country, through which they had marched, with an extensive chain of Cantonments. That link, which the post at Trenton supplied, consisted of a Hessian Brigade of Infantry, a Company of Chasseurs, a Squadron of Light Dragoons and six Field Pieces. At eight o'clock in the morning of the twenty-sixth of December, General Washington, with twenty-four hundred men, came upon them (after they had paraded) took one thousand prisoners, and repassed the same day without loss to his encampment. As soon as the troops were recovered from their excessive fatigue, General Washington recrossed a second time to Trenton. On the second of January, Lord Cornwallis with the bulk of the British army advanced upon him, cannonaded his post, and offered him battle: but, the two armies being separated by the interposition of Trenton Creek, General Washington had it in his option to decline an engagement; which he did for the sake of striking the masterly stroke that he then meditated. Having kindled frequent fires around his camp, posted faithful men to keep them burning, and advanced centinels whoſe fidelity might be relied upon, he decamped ſilently after dark, and, by a circuitous route, reached Princeton at 9 o' clock the next morning. The noiſe of the firing, by which he killed and captured between five and ſix hundred of the Britiſh Brigade in that town, was the firſt notice Lord Cornwallis had of this ſtolen march. General Waſhington, the project ſucceſsfully accomplisſhed, inſtantly filed off for the mountainous grounds of Morris Town. Mean while His Lordſhip, who arrived by a forced march at Princeton, juſt as he had left it, finding the Americans could not be overtaken, proceeded without halting to Brunſwick.

On the fifth of January 1777, from Pluckemin, General Waſhington diſpatched an account of this ſecond ſucceſs to General Putnam and ordered him to move immediately with all his troops to Croſſwix, for the purpoſe of co-operating in recovering the Jerſeys: an event which the preſent fortunate juncture (while the enemy were yet panic-ſtruck) appeared to promiſe. The General cautioned him, however, if the enemy ſhould ſtill continue at Brunſwick, to guard with great circumſpection againſt a ſurpriſe: eſpecially, as they, having recently ſuffered by two attacks, could ſcarcely avoid being edged with resentment to attempt retaliation. His Excellency farther advised him to give out his strength to be twice as great as it was; to forward on all the baggage and scattering men belonging to the Division destined for Morris Town; to employ as many spies as he should think proper; to keep a number of horsemen, in the dress of the country, going constantly backwards and forwards on the same secret service; and lastly, if he should discover any intention or motion of the enemy that could be depended upon and might be of consequence, not to fail in conveying the intelligence as rapidly as possible by express to Head Quarters. Major General Putnam was directed soon after to take post at Princeton; where he continued until the spring. He had never with him more than a few hundred troops, though he was only at fifteen miles distance from the enemy's strong garrison of Brunswick. At one period from a sudden diminution, occasioned by the tardiness of the militia, turning out to replace those whose time of service was expired, he had fewer men for duty than he had miles of frontier to guard. Nor was the Commander in Chief in a more eligible situation. It is true, that, while he had scarcely the semblance of an army, under the specious parade of a park of artillery and the imposing appearance of his Head Quarters, eſtabliſhed at Morris Town, he kept up in the eyes of his countrymen as well as in the opinion of his enemy, the appearance of no contemptible force. Future generations will find difficulty in conceiving how a handful of new-levied Men and Militia, who were neceſſitated to be inoculated for the Small-Pox in the courſe of the winter, could be ſubdivided and poſted ſo advantageouſly, as, effectually to protect the inhabitants, confine the enemy, curtail their forage, and beat up their quarters, without ſuſtaining a ſingle diſaſter.

In the battle of Princeton Capt. McPherſon, of the 17th Britiſh Regiment, a very worthy Scotchman, was deſperately wounded in the lungs and left with the dead. Upon General Putnam's arrival there, he found him languiſhing in extreme diſtreſs, without a ſurgeon, without a ſingle accommodation, and without a friend to ſolace the ſinking ſpirit in the gloomy hour of death. He viſited and immediately cauſed every poſſible comfort to be adminiſtered to him. Captain McPherſon, who contrary to all appearances recovered, after having demonſtrated to General Putnam the dignified ſenſe of obligations which a generous mind wiſhes not to conceal, one day in familiar converſation demanded—" pray, Sir,

" what countryman are you?"—" An Ame-
" rican," anſwered the latter.—" Not a Yan-
" kee?"—ſaid the other. " A full-blood-
" ed one," replied the General. " By G—d,
" I am ſorry for that," rejoined McPherſon,
" I did not think there could be ſo much good-
" neſs and generoſity in an American, or, in-
" deed in any body but a Scotchman."

WHILE the recovery of Captain McPherſon was doubtful, he deſired that General Putnam would permit a friend in the Britiſh army at Brunſwick to come and aſſiſt him in making HIS WILL. General Putnam, who had then only fifty men in his whole command, was ſadly embarraſſed by the propoſition. On the one hand, he was not content that a Britiſh Officer ſhould have an opportunity to ſpy out the weakneſs of his poſt—on the other, it was ſcarcely in his nature to refuſe complying with a dictate of humanity. He luckily bethought himſelf of an expedient, which he haſtened to put in practice. A Flag of Truce was diſpatched with Captain McPherſon's requeſt, but under an injunction not to return with his friend until after dark. In the evening lights were placed in all the rooms of the College, and in every apartment of the vacant houſes throughout the town. During the whole night, the fifty men, ſometimes all together and ſometimes in ſmall detachments, were marched from different quarters by the houſe in which McPherſon lay. Afterwards it was known, that the Officer who came on the viſit at his return reported, that General Putnam's Army upon the moſt moderate calculation could not conſiſt of leſs than four or five thouſand men.

THIS winter's campaign (for our troops conſtantly kept the field after regaining a footing in the Jerſeys) has never yet been faithfully and feelingly deſcribed. The ſudden reſtoration of our cauſe from the very verge of ruin, was interwoven with ſuch a tiſſue of inſcrutable cauſes and extraordinary events, that, fearful of doing the ſubject greater injuſtice by a paſſing diſquiſition than a purpoſed ſilence, I leave it to the leiſure of abler pens. The ill policy of the Britiſh doubtleſs contributed to accelerate this event. For the manner, impolitic as inhuman, in which they managed their temporary conqueſts tended evidently to alienate the affections of their adherents, to confirm the wavering in an oppoſite intereſt, to rouſe the ſupine into activity, to aſſemble the diſperſed to the Standard of America, and to infuſe a ſpirit of revolt into the minds of thoſe men, who had from neceſſity ſubmitted to their power. Their conduct in warring with fire and ſword againſt the imbecility of youth and the decrepitude of age; againſt the Arts, the Sciences, the curious Inventions and the elegant improvements in civilized life; againſt the melancholy Widow, the miſerable Orphan, the peaceable profeſſor of humane Literature, and the ſacred Miniſter of the Goſpel, ſeemed to operate as powerfully, as if purpoſely intended to kindle the dormant ſpark of reſiſtance into an inextinguiſhable flame. If we add, to the black catalogue of provocations already enumerated, their inſatiable rapacity in plundering friends and foes indiſcriminately; their libidinous brutality in violating the chaſtity of the female ſex, their more than Gothic rage in defacing private Writings, public Records, Libraries of learning, Dwellings of individuals, Edifices for education and Temples of the Deity; together with their inſufferable ferocity (unprecedented indeed among civilized nations) in murdering on the field of battle the wounded while begging for mercy, in cauſing their priſoners to famiſh with hunger and cold in Priſons and Priſon-Ships, and in carrying their malice beyond death itſelf by denying the decent rites of ſepulture to the dead,—we ſhall not be aſtoniſhed that the Yeomanry in the two Jerſeys, when the firſt glimmering of hope began to break in upon them, rose as one man, with the unalterable resolution to perish in the generous cause or expel their merciless invaders.

The principal Officers, stationed at a variety of well-chosen and at some almost inaccessible positions, seemed all to be actuated by the same soul and only to vie with each other in giving proofs of vigilance, enterprize and valour. From what has been said respecting the scantiness of our aggregate force, it will be concluded that the number of men, under the orders of each, was indeed very small. But the uncommon alertness of the troops who were incessantly hovering round the enemy in scouts, and the constant communication, they kept between the several stations most contiguous to each other (agreeably to the † Instructions of the General in

† The annexed private Orders to Lord Stirling will shew, in a laconic and military manner, the system of service then pursued.

" To Brigadier General Lord Stirling.

" My Lord,

" You are to repair to Baskenridge and take upon you the command of the troops now there, and such as may be sent to your care.

" You are to endeavour, as much as possible, to harrass and annoy the enemy by keeping scouting parties constantly (or as frequently as possible) around their

Chief) together with their readineſs in giving and confidence of receiving ſuch reciprocal aid as the exigencies might require, ſerv'ed to ſupply the defect of force.

This manner of doing duty not only put our own poſts beyond the reach of ſudden inſult, and ſurprize; but ſo exceedingly harraſſed and intimidated the enemy that foragers were ſeldom ſent out by them, and never except in very large parties. General Dickenſon, who commanded on General Putnam's left, diſcovered about the 20th of January, a foraging party conſiſting of about four hundred men, on the oppoſite ſide of the *Mill-Stone*,

" As you will be in the neighbourhood of Generals Dickenſon and Warner, I recommend it to you, to keep up a correſpondence with them, and endeavour to regulate your parties by theirs ſo as to have ſome conſtantly out.

" Uſe every means in your power to obtain intelligence from the enemy; which may poſſibly be better effected by engaging ſome of thoſe people who have obtained *Protections* to go in, under pretence of aſking advice, than by any other means.

" You will alſo uſe every means in your power to obtain and communicate the earlieſt accounts of the enemy's movements; and to aſſemble, in the ſpeedieſt manner poſſible, your troops either for offence or defence.

Given *at Head Quarters*
the fourth day of February 1777.
Geo. Washington."

two miles from Somerſet court-houſe. As the bridge was poſſeſſed and defended by three field pieces ſo that it could not be paſſed; General Dickenſon, at the head of four hundred militia, broke the ice, croſſed the river (where the water was about three feet deep) reſolutely attacked and totally defeated the foragers. Upon their abandoning the convoy, a few priſoners, forty waggons, and more than a hundred draft horſes with a conſiderable booty of cattle and ſheep fell into his hands.

Nor were our operations on General Putnam's right flank leſs fortunate. To give countenance to the numerous friends of the Britiſh Government in the county of Monmouth, appears to have been a principal motive with Sir William Howe for ſtretching the chain of his cantonments (by his own * confeſſion previouſly to his diſaſter) rather

* Extract of a letter from General Sir William Howe, to Lord George Germaine, dated New-York, December 20, 1776.

Having mentioned the fruitleſs attempt of Lord Cornwallis to find boats at Corryel's ferry to paſs the Delaware—he proceeds thus:

"The paſſage of the Delaware being thus rendered impracticable, his Lordſhip took poſt at Pennington, in which place and Trenton the two diviſions remained until the fourteenth, when the weather having become too ſevere to keep the field, and the winter cantonments be-too far. After that chain became broken, as I have already related, by the blows at Trenton and Princeton, he was obliged to collect during the rest of the winter the useless remains in his barracks at Brunswick. In the meantime General Putman was much more successful in his attempt to protect our dispersed and dispirited friends in the same district; who, environed on every side by envenomed adversaries remained inseparably rivetted in affection to American Independence. He first detached Colonel Guerny and afterwards Major* Davis, with such parties of

ing arranged, the troops marched from both places to their respective stations. *The chain, I own, is rather too extensive*, but I was induced to occupy Burlington to cover the County of Monmouth, in which there are many loyal inhabitants; and trusting to the almost general submission of the Country to the southward of this chain, and to the strength of the Corps placed in the advanced posts, I conclude the troops will be in perfect security."

* As there happened to be in my possession a copy of one of his letters to those Officers, it was thought worthy of insertion here, in order to demonstrate his satisfaction with their conduct:

" To Major John Davis, of the third Battalion of Cumberland County Militia.

" SIR,

" I am much obliged to you for your activity, vigor and diligence since you have been under my command: you will, therefore, march your men to Philadelphia and there discharge them; returning into the store all the militia as could be ſpared, for their ſupport. Several ſkirmiſhes enſued in which our people had always the advantage. They took, at different times, many priſoners, horſes and waggons from foraging parties. In effect ſo well did they cover the country as to induce ſome of the moſt reſpectable inhabitants to declare, that the ſecurity of the perſons, as well as the ſalvation of the property of many friends to freedom, was owing to the ſpirited exertions of theſe two detachments: who at the ſame time that they reſcued the county from the tyranny of Tories, afforded an opportunity for the militia to recover from their conſternation, to embody themſelves in warlike array and to ſtand on their defence.

During this period General Putnam having received unqueſtionable intelligence, that a party of Refugees in Britiſh pay had taken poſt and were erecting a kind of Redoubt at Lawrence's Neck, ſent Colonel Nelſon with one hundred and fifty militia to ſurprize them. That officer conducted with ſo much ſecrecy and deciſion as to take the whole priſoners.

ammunition, arms and accoutrements, you received at that place.

I am, Sir, your humble Servant

Israel Putnam.

Princeton February 5th, 1777.

These * Refugees commanded by Major Stockton, belonging to Skinner's Brigade and amounted to ſixty in number.

A SHORT time after this event, Lord Cornwallis ſent out another foraging party towards Bound-Brook. General Putnam, having received notice from his emiſſaries, detached Major Smith with a few Riflemen to annoy the party and followed himſelf with the reſt of his force. Before he could come up, Major Smith, who had formed an ambuſh, attacked the enemy, killed ſeveral horſes, took a few priſoners and ſixteen baggage-waggons, without ſuſtaining any injury. By ſuch operations, our hero, in the courſe of the winter, captured nearly a thouſand priſoners.

IN the latter part of February General Waſhington adviſed General Putnam, that, in

* Extract of a Letter from General Putnam to the Council of Safety of Pennſylvania, dated at Princeton February 18th, 1777.

" Yeſterday evening Colonel Nelſon, with a hundred " and fifty men, at Laurence's Neck, attacked ſixty " men of Cortland Skinner's Brigade, commanded by " the enemy's RENOWNED LAND PILOT *Major Richard Stockton*, routed them and took the whole priſoners—among them the Major, a Captain and three Subalterns, with ſeventy ſtand of Arms. *Fifty of the* " *Bedford Pennſylvania Riflemen behaved like veterans.*"

consequence of a large accession of strength from New-York to the British army at Brunswick, it was to be apprehended they would soon make a forward movement towards the Delaware: in which case the latter was directed to cross the river with his actual force, to assume the command of the Militia who might assemble, to secure the boats on the west side of the Delaware and to facilitate the passage of the rest of the army. But the enemy did not remove from their winter-quarters until the season arrived when green forage could be supplied. In the intermediate period, the correspondence on the part of General Putnam with the Commander in Chief consisted principally of reports and enquiries concerning the treatment of some of the following descriptions of persons: either of those who came within our lines with flags and pretended flags, or who had taken protection from the enemy, or who had been reputed disaffected to our cause, or who were designed to be comprehended in the American Proclamation, which required that those who had taken protections should give them to the nearest American Officer, or go within the British lines. The letters of his Excellency in return, generally advisory, were indicative of confidence and approbation.

When the Spring had now ſo far advanced that it was obvious the enemy would ſoon take the field; the Commander in Chief, after deſiring General Putnam to give the officer who was to relieve him at Princeton all the information neceſſary for the conduct of that poſt, appointed that General to the command of a ſeparate Army in the Highlands of New-York.

It is ſcarcely decided, from any documents yet publiſhed, whether the prepoſterous plans proſecuted by the Britiſh Generals in the Campaign of 1777, were altogether the reſult of their Orders from home, or whether they partially originated from the contingences of the moment. The ſyſtem, which, at the time, tended to puzzle all human conjecture, when developed ſerved, alſo, to contradict all reaſonable calculation. Certain it is the American Commander in Chief was for a conſiderable time ſo perplexed with contradictory appearances, that he knew not how to diſtribute his troops, with his uſual diſcernment, ſo as to oppoſe the enemy with equal proſpect of ſucceſs in different parts. The gathering tempeſts menaced the northern Frontiers, the poſts in the Highlands and the City of Philadelphia: but it was ſtill doubtful where the fury of the ſtorm would fall.

At one time Sir William Howe was forcing his way by land to Philadelphia, at another relinquiſhing the Jerſeys, at a third facing round to make a ſudden inroad, then embarking with all the forces that could be ſpared from New-York, and then putting out to ſea —at the very moment when General Burgoyne had reduced Ticonderoga, and ſeemed to require a co-operation in another quarter.

On our ſide, we have ſeen that the old Continental Army expired with the year 1776: ſince which, invention had been tortured with expedients and zeal with efforts to levy another. For on the ſucceſs of the recruiting ſervice depended the ſalvation of the country. The ſucceſs was ſuch as not to puff us up to preſumption, or depreſs us to deſpair. The army in the Jerſeys, under the orders of the General in Chief, conſiſted of all the troops raiſed ſouth of the Hudſon: that in the northern department, of the New-Hampſhire Brigade, two Brigades of Maſſachuſetts and the Brigade of New-York, together with ſome irregular Corps: and that in the Highlands of the remaining two Brigades of Maſſachuſetts, the Connecticut Line conſiſting two Brigades, the Brigade of Rhode-Iſland and one Regiment of New-

York. Upon hearing of the loſs of Ticonderoga and the progreſs of the Britiſh towards Albany, General Waſhington ordered the northern army to be reinforced with the two Brigades of Maſſachuſetts then in the Highlands—and, upon finding the army under his immediate command outnumbered by that of Sir William Howe, which had by the circuitous route of the Cheſapeak invaded Pennſylvania, he alſo called from the Highlands one of the Connecticut Brigades and that of Rhode-Iſland to his own aſſiſtance.

In the neighborhood of General Putnam there was no enemy capable of exciting alarms. The army left at New-York ſeemed only deſigned for its defence. In it were ſeveral entire Corps, compoſed of Tories who had flocked to the Britiſh ſtandard. There was, beſides, a band of lurking miſcreants, not properly enrolled, who ſtaid chiefly at Weſt Cheſter: from whence they infeſted the Country between the two armies, pillaged the cattle and carried off the peaceable inhabitants. It was an unworthy policy in Britiſh Generals to patronize Banditti. The Whig inhabitants on the edge of our lines and ſtill lower down, who had been plundered in a merciless manner, delayed not to ſtrip the Tories in return. People, moſt nearly connected and allied, frequently became moſt exaſperated and inveterate in malice. Then the ties of fellowſhip were broken—then, friendſhip itſelf being ſoured to enmity, the mind readily gave way to private revenge, uncontrouled retaliation and all the deforming paſſions that diſgrace humanity. Enormities, almoſt without a name, were perpetrated—at the deſcription of which, the boſom, not frozen to apathy, muſt glow with a mixture of pity and indignation. To prevent the predatory incurſions from below and to cover the County of Weſt Cheſter, General Putnam detached from his Head-Quarters, at Peeks-Kill, Meigs's Regiment, which in the courſe of the Campaign ſtruck ſeveral partizan ſtrokes and atchieved the objects for which it was ſent. He likewiſe took meaſures, without noiſe or oſtentation, to ſecure himſelf from being ſurpriſed and carried within the Britiſh lines by the Tories, who had formed a plan for the purpoſe. The information of this intended enterprize, conveyed to him through ſeveral channels, was corroborated by that obtained and tranſmitted by the Commander in Chief.

It was not wonderful that many of theſe Tories were able, undiſcovered, to penetrate far into the country and even to go with letters or meſſages from one Britiſh Army to another. The inhabitants, who were well affected to the royal cause, afforded them every possible support and their own knowledge of the different routes gave them a farther facility in performing their peregrinations. Sometimes the most active Loyalists (as the Tories wished to denominate themselves) who had gone into the British Posts and received promises of Commissions upon enlisting a certain number of Soldiers, came back again secretly with Recruiting Instructions. Sometimes these and others who came from the enemy within the verge of our Camps, were detected and condemned to death in conformity to the usages of war. But the British Generals, who had an unlimited supply of money at their command, were able to pay with so much liberality, that emissaries could always be found. Still, it is thought that the intelligence of the American Commanders, was, at least, equally accurate; notwithstanding the poverty of their military chest and the inability of rewarding mercenary agents, for secret services, in proportion to their risque and merit.

A PERSON by the name of Palmer, who was a Lieutenant in the Tory new Levies, was detected in the Camp at Peeks Kill. Governor Tryon, who commanded the new Levies, reclaimed him as a British Officer, represented the heinous crime of condemning a man commissioned by his Majesty and threatened vengeance in case he should be executed. General Putnam wrote the following pithy reply.

"SIR,

"NATHAN PALMER, a Lieutenant in
"your King's service, was taken in my
"Camp as a *Spy*—he was tried as a *Spy*—he
"was condemned as a *Spy*—and you may
"rest assured, Sir, he shall be hanged as a
"*Spy*.

I have the honor to be, &c.

ISRAEL PUTNAM."

"*His Excellency, Governor Tryon.*"

"P. S. Afternoon.
"He is hanged."

IMPORTANT transactions soon occurred. Not long after the two Brigades had marched from Peeks Kill to Pennsylvania, a reinforcement arrived at New-York from Europe. Appearances indicated that offensive operations would follow. General Putnam, having been reduced in force to a single Brigade in the field and a single Regiment in garrison at Fort Montgomery, repeatedly informed the Commander in Chief that the poſts committed to his charge muſt in all probability be loſt, in caſe an attempt ſhould be made upon them; and that, circumſtanced as he was, he could not be reſponſible for the conſequences. His ſituation was certainly to be lamentéd, but it was not in the power of the Commander in Chief to alter it: except by authoriſing him to call upon the Militia for aid —an aid always precarious; and often ſo tardy, as when obtained to be of no utility.

On the fifth of October, Sir Henry Clinton came up the North River with three thouſand men. After making many feints to miſlead the attention, he landed, the next morning, at Stoney Point and commenced his march over the mountains to Fort Montgomery. Governor Clinton, an active, reſolute and intelligent officer, who commanded the Garriſon, upon being appriſed of the movement, diſpatched a letter by expreſs to General Putnam for ſuccour. By the treachery of the meſſenger the letter miſcarried. General Putnam, aſtoniſhed at hearing nothing reſpecting the enemy, rode, with General Parſons and Colonel Root his Adjutant General, to reconnoitre them at Kings Ferry. In the mean time, at five o'clock in the afternoon, Sir Henry Clinton's columns, having ſurmounted the obſtacles and barriers of nature, deſcended from the Thunder-Hill, through thickets impaſſable but for light troops and * attacked the different redoubts.

* The Author of theſe Memoirs, then Major of Brigade to the firſt Connecticut Brigade, was alone at Head-Quarters when the firing began. He haſtened to Colonel Wyllys, the ſenior officer in camp and adviſed him to diſpatch all the men not on duty to Fort Montgomery, without waiting for orders. About five hundred men marched inſtantly under Colonel Meigs; and the author, with Doctor Beardſley, a Surgeon in the Brigade, rode at full ſpeed through a bye-path, to let the garriſon know, that a reinforcement was on its march. Notwithſtanding all the haſte theſe officers made to and over the river, the Fort was ſo completely inveſted, on their arrival, that it was impoſſible to enter. They went on board the new Frigate, which lay near the fortreſs, and had the misfortune to be idle, though not unconcerned, ſpectators of the ſtorm. They ſaw the minuteſt actions diſtinctly when the works were carried. The Frigate, after receiving ſeveral platoons, ſlipped her cable and proceeded a little way up the river: but the wind and tide becoming adverſe, the crew ſet her on fire, to prevent her falling into the hands of the enemy; whoſe ſhips were approaching.—The louring darkneſs of the night, the profound ſtillneſs that reigned, the interrupted flaſhes of the flames that illuminated the waters, the long ſhadows of the cliffs that now and then were ſeen, the exploſion of the cannon which were left loaded in the ſhip, and the reverberating echo which reſounded, at intervals, between the ſtupendous mountains on both ſides of the river, compoſed an awful night piece, for perſons prepared (by the preceding ſcene) to contemplate ſubjects of horrid ſublimity.

The garrison, inspired by the conduct of their leaders, defended the works with distinguished valor. But, as the post had been designed principally to prevent the passing of ships and as an assault in rear had not been expected, the works on the land side were incomplete and untenable. In the dusk of twilight the British entered with their bayonets fixed. Their loss was inconsiderable. Nor was that of the garrison great. Governor Clinton, his brother General James Clinton, Colonel Dubois, and most of the officers and men effected their escape under cover of the thick smoke and darkness that suddenly prevailed. The capture of this fort by Sir Henry Clinton, together with the consequent removal of the chains andbooms that obstructed the navigation, opened a passage to Albany and seemed to favor a junction of his force with that of General Burgoyne. But the latter having been compelled to capitulate a few days after this event, and great numbers of Militia having arrived from New-England, the successful army returned to New-York—yet not before a detachment from it, under the Orders of General Vaughan, had burnt the defenceless town of Esopus, and several scattering buildings on the banks of the river.

NOTWITHSTANDING the army in the Highlands had been ſo much weakened (for the ſake of ſtrengthening the armies in other quarters) as to have occaſioned the loſs of Fort Montgomery, yet that loſs was productive of no conſequences. Our main army in Pennſylvania, after having contended with ſuperior force in two indeciſive battles, ſtill held the enemy in check. While the ſplendid ſucceſs, which attended our arms at the Northward, gave a more favorable aſpect to the American affairs, at the cloſe of this campaign, than they had ever before aſſumed.

When the enemy fell back to New-York by water, we followed them a part of the way by land. Colonel Meigs, with a detachment from the ſeveral Regiments in General Parſons's Brigade, having made a forced march from Crompond to Weſt-Cheſter, ſurpriſed and broke up for a time the band of freebooters: of whom he brought off fifty, together with many Cattle and Horſes which they had recently ſtolen.

Soon after this enterprize, General Putnam advanced towards the Britiſh lines. As he had received intelligence that ſmall bodies of the enemy were out with orders from Governor Tryon to burn Wright's Mills, he prevented it by detaching three parties of one hundred men in each. One of these parties fell in with and captured thirty-five; and another forty of the New Levies. But as he could not prevent a third hostile party from burning the house of Mr. Van Tassel, a noted Whig and a Committee man, who was forced to go along with them, naked and barefoot, on the icy ground, in a freezing night: he, for the professed purpose of retaliation, sent Captain Buchanan, in a Whale-boat, to burn the house of General Oliver Delancey on York Island. Buchanan effected his object, and by this expedition put a period for the present to that unmeaning and wanton species of destruction.

While General Putnam quartered at New Rochel, a scouting party which had been sent to West Farms, below West-Chester, surrounded the house in which Colonel James Delancey lodged, and, notwithstanding he crept under the bed the better to be concealed, brought him to Head-Quarters before morning. This Officer was exchanged by the British General without delay, and placed at the head of the Cow-Boys, a licentious Corps of irregulars, who, in the sequel, committed unheard-of depredations and excesses.

It was distressing to see so beautiful a part

of the country ſo barbarouſly waſted; and, often to witneſs ſome peculiar ſcene of female miſery. For moſt of the female inhabitants had been obliged to fly within the lines poſſeſſed by one army or the other. Near our quarters was an affecting inſtance of human viciſſitude. Mr. William Sutton of Maroneck, an inoffenſive man, a merchant by profeſſion, who lived in a decent faſhion and whoſe family had as happy proſpects as almoſt any in the country, upon ſome imputation of Toryiſm went to the enemy. His wife, oppreſſed with grief in her diſagreeable ſtate of dereliction, did not long ſurvive. Betſey Sutton, their eldeſt daughter, was a modeſt and lovely young woman, of about fifteen years old, when at the death of her mother, the care of five or ſix younger children devolved upon her. She was diſcreet and provident beyond her years. But when we ſaw her, ſhe looked to be feeble in health—broken in ſpirit—wan, melancholy, and dejected. She ſaid " that their laſt cow, which furniſhed " milk for the children, had lately been taken away—that they had frequently been " plundered of their wearing apparel and furniture, ſhe believed, by both parties—that " they had little more to loſe—and that ſhe " knew not where to procure bread for the " dear little ones, who had no father to pro-

"vide for them"—*no mother*—ſhe was going to have ſaid—but a torrent of tears choaked articulation. In coming to that part of the country, again, after ſome campaigns had elapſed, I found the habitation deſolate and the garden overgrown with weeds. Upon enquiry I learnt, that, as ſoon as we left the place, ſome ruffians broke into the houſe, while ſhe lay in bed, in the latter part of the night: and that, having been terrified by their rudeneſs, ſhe ran half-naked into a neighboring ſwamp, where ſhe continued until the morning—there the poor girl caught a violent cold, which ended in a conſumption. It finiſhed a life without a ſpot—and a career of ſufferings commenced and continued without a fault.

Sights of wretchedneſs always touched with commiſeration the feelings of General Putnam and prompted his generous ſoul to ſuccour the afflicted. But the indulgence, which he ſhewed (whenever it did not militate againſt his duty) towards the deſerted and ſuffering families of the Tories in the State of New-York, was the cauſe of his becoming unpopular with no inconſiderable claſs of people in that State. On the other ſide, he had conceived an unconquerable averſion to many of the perſons, who were entruſted with the difpofal of Tory-property, becaufe he believ-ed them to have been guilty of peculations and other infamous practices. But, although the enmity between him and the Sequeftrators' was acrimonious as mutual; yet he lived in habits of amity with the moft refpectable characters in public departments as well as in private life.

His character was alfo refpected by the enemy. He had been acquainted with many of the principal Officers in a former war. As flags frequently paffed between the out-pofts, during his continuance on the lines, it was a common practice to forward News-Papers by them; and as thofe printed by Rivington, the Royal Printer in New-York, were infamous for the falfehoods with which they abounded, General Putnam once fent a Packet to his old friend General Robertfon with this Billet: "Major General Putnam pre-"fents his Compliments to Major General "Robertfon and fends him fome American "News-Papers for his perufal—when Gen-"eral Robertfon fhall have done with them, "it is requefted they be given to Rivington, "in order that he may print fome truth."

Late in the year we left the lines and repaired to the Highlands. For upon the lofs of fort Montgomery, the Commander in Cheif determined to build another fortification for the defence of the river. His Excellency, accordingly, wrote to General Putman to fix upon the ſpot. After reconnoitering all the different places propoſed, and revolving in his own mind their relative advantages for offence on the water and defence on the land, he fixed upon WEST POINT. It is no vulgar praiſe to ſay, that to him belongs the glory of having choſen this rock of our military ſalvation. The poſition for water batteries, which might ſweep the channel where the river formed a right angle, made it the moſt proper of any for commanding the navigation; while the rocky ridges, that roſe in awful ſublimity behind each other, rendered it impregnable, and even incapable of being inveſted by leſs than twenty thouſand men. The Britiſh, who conſidered this poſt as a ſort of American Gibraltar, never attempted it but by the treachery of an American officer. All the world knows that this project failed and that Weſt Point, continues to be the receptacle of every thing valuable in military preparations to the preſent day.

IN the month of January 1778, when a ſnow two feet deep lay on the earth, General

Parſons's Brigade went to Weſt Point and broke ground. Want of covering for the troops, together with want of tools and materials for the works, made the proſpect truly gloomy and diſcouraging. It was neceſſary that means ſhould be found, though our currency was depreciated and our treaſury exhauſted. The eſtimates and requiſitions of Colonel la Radiere, the Engineer who laid out the works, altogether diſproportioned to our circumſtances, ſerved only to put us in mind of our poverty, and, as it were, to ſatirize our reſources. His petulant behaviour and unaccommodating diſpoſition added further embarraſsments. It was then that the patriotiſm of Governor Clinton ſhone in full luſtre. His exertions to furniſh ſupplies can never be too much commended. His influence, ariſing from his popularity, was unlimited: yet he heſitated not to put all his popularity at riſque, whenever the federal intereſts demanded. Notwithſtanding the impediments that oppoſed our progreſs, with his aid before the opening of the campaign, the works were in great forwardneſs.

According to a reſolution of Congreſs, an enquiry was to be made into the cauſes of military diſaſters. Major General McDougall, Brigadier General Huntington and Colonel

Wigglefworth compofed the Court of Enquiry on the lofs of fort Montgomery. Upon full knowledge and mature deliberation of facts on the fpot, they reported the lofs to have been occafioned by want of men and not by any fault in the Commanders.

General Putnam, who during the inveftigation, was relieved from duty, as foon as Congrefs had approved the Report, took command of the right Wing of the Grand Army, under the Orders of the General in Chief. This was juft after the Battle of Monmouth, when the three armies which had, laft year, acted feparately, joined at the White Plains. Our effective force, in one camp was at no other time fo refpectable as at this juncture. The army confifted of fixty regular Regiments of foot formed into fifteen Brigades, four Battalions of Artillery, four Regiments of Horfe and feveral Corps of State Troops. But as the enemy kept clofe within their Lines on York-Ifland, nothing could be attempted. Towards the end of Autumn, we broke up the Camp, and went firft to Fredericksburg, and thence to winter quarters.

In order to cover the Country adjoining to the *Sound* and to fupport the garrifon of *Weft*

Point, in caſe of an attack, Major General Putnam was ſtationed for the winter at Reading in Connecticut. He had under his Orders the Brigade of New-Hampſhire, the two Brigades of Connecticut, the Corps of Infantry commanded by Hazen and that of Cavalry by Sheldon.

The troops, who had been badly fed, badly cloathed and worſe paid, by brooding over their grievances in the leiſure and inactivity of winter-quarters began to think them intolerable. The Connecticut Brigades formed the deſign of marching to Hartford, where the General Aſſembly was then in Seſſion, and of demanding redreſs at the point of the Bayonet. Word having been brought to General Putnam that the ſecond Brigade was under arms for this purpoſe, he mounted his horſe, galloped to the Cantonment and thus addreſſed them: " My brave lads, whither " are you going? Do you intend to deſert " your Officers and to invite the enemy to " follow you into the country? Whoſe cauſe " have you been fighting and ſuffering ſo " long in, is it not your own? Have you no " property, no parents, wives or children? " You have behaved like men ſo far—all the " world is full of your praiſes—and poſterity " will ſtand aſtoniſhed at your deeds: but

"not if you ſpoil all at laſt. Don't you con-
"ſider how much the country is diſtreſſed by
"the war, and that your officers have not
"been any better paid than yourſelves? But
"we all expect better times and that the
"Country will do us ample juſtice. Let us
"all ſtand by one another then and fight it
"out like brave Soldiers. Think what a
"ſhame it would be for Connecticut-men to
"run away from their Officers."—After the ſeveral Regiments had received the General as he rode along the line *with drums beating and preſented arms*; the Sergeants, who had then the command, brought the men *to an Order*, in which poſition they continued while he was ſpeaking. When he had done, he directed the acting Major of Brigade to give the word for them to ſhoulder, march to their Regimental parades and lodge arms. All which they executed with promtitude and apparent good humour. One Soldier only, who had been the moſt active, was confined in the quarter-guard: from whence, at night, he attempted to make his eſcape. But the centinel, who had alſo been in the mutiny, ſhot him dead on the ſpot, and thus the affair ſubſided.

About the middle of winter, while General Putnam was on a viſit to his out-poſt at Horse-Neck, he found Governor Tryon advancing upon that town with a corps of fifteen hundred men—to oppose these, General Putnam had only a Picket of one hundred and fifty men and two iron field pieces without horses or drag-ropes. He, however, planted his cannon on the high ground by the meeting-house, and retarded their approach by firing several times, until, perceiving the horse (supported by the infantry) about to charge, he ordered the picket to provide for their safety by retiring to a swamp inaccessible to horse; and secured his own by plunging down the steep precipice at the church upon a full trot. This precipice is so steep, where he descended, as to have artificial stairs composed of nearly one hundred stone-steps for the accommodation of foot passengers, There the Dragoons, who were but a swords' length from him, stopped short. For the declivity was so abrupt that they ventured not to follow: and, before they could gain the valley by going round the brow of the hill in the ordinary road, he was far enough beyond their reach. He continued his route unmolested to Stamford, from whence, having strengthened his picket by the junction of some militia, he came back again, and in turn, pursued Governor Tryon in his retreat. As he rode down the precipice, one ball, of the many fired at him, went through his beaver. But Governor Tryon, by way of compenſation for ſpoiling his hat, ſent him ſoon afterwards, as a preſent, a complete ſuit of Cloaths.*

In the Campaign of 1779, which terminated the career of General Putnam's ſervices, he commanded the Maryland line poſted at Butter-milk falls, about two miles below Weſt Point. He was happy in poſſeſſing the friendſhip of the officers of that Line and in living on terms of hoſpitality with them. Indeed there was no family in the army that lived better than his own. The General, his ſecond ſon Major Daniel Putnam, and the writer of theſe Memoirs compoſed that family. This campaign, principally ſpent in ſtrengthening the works of Weſt Point, was only ſignaliſed for the ſtorm of Stoney-Point by the Light Infantry under the conduct of General Wayne, and the ſurpriſe of the poſt of Powles Hook by the Corps under the command of Colonel Henry Lee. When the army quitted the field and marched to Morris Town into winter quarters, General Putnam's family went into Connecticut for a few weeks. In December, the General began his journey to Morris Town. Upon the road between Pomfret and Hartford he felt an unufual torpor flowly pervading his right hand and foot. This heavinefs crept gradually on, and untill it had deprived him of the ufe of his limbs on that fide, in a confiderable degree, before he reached the houfe of his friend Colonel Wadfworth. Still he was unwilling to confider his diforder of the paralytic kind and endeavoured to fhake it off by exertion. Having found that impoffible, a temporary dejection, difguifed however under a veil of affumed chearfulnefs, fucceeded. But reafon, philofophy, and religion foon reconciled him to his fate. In that fituation he has conftantly remained, favored with fuch a portion of bodily activity as enables him to walk and to ride moderately; and retaining unimpaired his relifh for enjoyment, his love of pleafantry, his ftrength of memory and all the faculties of his mind. As a proof that the powers of memory are not weakened, it ought to be obferved, that he has lately repeated from recollection all the adventures of his life, which are here recorded, and which had formerly been communicated to the compiler in detached converfations.

In patient yet fearlefs expectation of the approach of THE KING OF TERRORS, whom he hath full often faced in the field of blood, the Chriftian hero now enjoys in domeftic retirement the fruit of his early induftry. Having in youth provided a competent fubfiftence for old age, he was fecured from the danger of penury and diftrefs, to which, fo many Officers and Soldiers worn out in the public fervice have been reduced. To illuftrate his merits the more fully, this Effay will be concluded with a copy of the laft letter written to him, by General Wafhington, in his military character.

Head-Quarters, 2d June, 1783.

" Dear Sir,

" Your favor of the 20th of May I receiv-
" ed with much pleafure. For I can affure
" you that among the many worthy and me-
" ritorious Officers, with whom I have had
" the happinefs to be connected in fervice
" through the courfe of this war, and from
" whofe cheerful affiftance in the various and
" trying viciffitudes of a complicated conteft,
" *the name of a* Putnam *is not forgotten*: nor
" will be, but with that ftroke of time which
" fhall obliterate from my mind the remem-
" brance of all thofe toils and fatigues,
" through which we have ftruggled for the
" prefervation and eftablifhment of the

"*Rights, Liberties* and *Independence* of our
" *Country*.

" YOUR congratulations on the happy
" prospects of Peace and Independent secu-
" rity, with their attendant blessings to the
" UNITED STATES, I receive with great sa-
" tisfaction; and beg that you will accept a
" return of my gratulations to you on this
" auspicious event—an event, in which,
" great as it is in itself and glorious as it
" will probably be in its consequences, you
" have a right to participate largely, from
" the distinguished part you have contribu-
" ted towards its attainment.

" But while I contemplate the greatness
" of the object for which we have contended,
" and felicitate you on the happy issue of our
" toils and labours, which have terminated
" with such general satisfaction; I lament
" that you should feel the ungrateful returns
" of a Country, in whose service you have
" exhausted your bodily strength and expen-
" ded the vigour of a youthful constitution.
" I wish however, that your expectations of
" returning liberality may be verified. I
" have a hope they may:—but should they
" not, your case will not be a singular one. *In-*
" *gratitude has been experienced in all ages,*

" and Republics *in particular, have ever
" been famed for the exercise of that unnatural
" and* SORDID VICE.

" The Secretary at War, who is now
" here, informs me that you have ever been
" considered as entitled to full pay, since
" your absence from the field; and that you
" will still be considered in that light untill
" the close of the war: at which period you
" will be equally entitled to the same emolu-
" ments of half-pay or commutation, as other
" officers of your rank. The same opinion
" is also given by the Pay Master General,
" who is now with the army, impowered by
" Mr. Morris for the settlement of all their
" accounts, and who will attend to your's
" whenever you shall think proper to send
" on for the purpose; which it will proba-
" bly be best for you to do in a short time.

" I anticipate, with pleasure, the day
" (and that I trust not far off) when I shall
" quit the busy scenes of a military employ-
" ment, and retire to the more tranquil walks
" of domestic life. In that, or whatever other
" situation Providence may dispose of my
" future days, THE REMEMBRANCE OF THE
" MANY FRIENDSHIPS AND CONNECTIONS I
" HAVE HAD THE HAPPINESS TO CONTRACT

" WITH THE GENTLEMEN OF THE ARMY,
" WILL BE ONE OF MY MOST GRATEFUL RE-
" FLECTIONS. *Under this contemplation, and
" impressed with the sentiments of benevolence
" and regard, I commend you, my dear Sir, my
" other friends, and, with them, the interests
" and happiness of our dear Country to the*
" KEEPING AND PROTECTION OF ALMIGHTY
" GOD."

I have the honor to be, &c.
GEORGE WASHINGTON.

To the Honorable
Major General Putnam.

www.ingramcontent.com/pod-product-compliance
Lightning Source LLC
Chambersburg PA
CBHW031110020726
47495CB00007B/2128

* 9 7 8 3 3 3 7 0 8 7 4 3 2 *